BEHIND THE Tangerine Door

Tricia Daniels

New Series from Award-Winning Romance
Author Tricia Daniels

There is no place more beautiful to me than the home I've made with the love of my life. We're surrounded by rushing waters, rugged landscapes, rolling hills and magnificent views. Where people are real, and life doesn't have to be perfect to be wonderful. It's the most magnificent inspiration for love. Set in the communities that form the Headwaters, the 'Love in the Hills of the Headwaters Series' will bring you stories you can relate to; people you can connect with; and love you can believe in. It's the perfect place for city glam to meet country charm. Come Join us in the Hills of the Headwaters and find a place to explore, unplug and fall in love.

Disclaimer

This book is a work of fiction. All characters, places, and events are from the author's imagination and should not be confused with fact. Any resemblance to persons, living or dead, events or places, is purely coincidental.

Acknowledgements

Special Thank you to the Town of Mono, and the surrounding communities of the Headwaters for their endless inspiration.

Editing by Karen Hrdlicka of Barren Acres Editing
Cover Design by JM Walker - Just Write Creations

CHAPTER ONE

I'm startled awake by the tousling of the aircraft as it attempts a subtle landing at Toronto's Pearson International Airport. My short power nap during the flight was the first time I've slept in days. Normally, I'd be aggravated by the impatient people who unclip their seat belts, and stand in the aisles, before the plane comes to a complete stop.

Why they feel it's necessary to drag down their heavy baggage, knocking people in the head, and crowding everyone else before the first twenty-seven rows have started to exit, I have no idea.

Today I couldn't care less if every last one of them beats me to the long line-up in customs. They can rush, but we're all going to meet up again at the luggage carousel regardless. I'll just stay put in my seat until I'm the last one left on the plane. I'm in no hurry to face the situation that's brought me back to Canada and getting home five minutes earlier isn't going to change anything. I stare out the window, watching the airport crew do their thing out on the tarmac. In the torrential rain, they hurriedly toss each bag, one by one, onto the awaiting luggage transport cart. I hope the ancient travel trunk, which belonged to my mother, stands up to the weather.

The drive from the airport is miserable, pretty much mirroring my mood. It's as if I've been followed by a dark cloud ever since I got *the call*. The rain pounds so hard against the windshield that the wipers are almost ineffective against the driving force. After a stormy, hour-long drive on rain-soaked roads, I lean forward so I can talk to the driver. "Be careful," I warn. "This road washes out in places."

He makes a cautious turn onto the gravel country road then hits the gas, making the wheels spin. I grab onto the seat as the car fishtails in the mud. The driver looks at me apologetically in the rearview mirror and I shake my head. It's been several years since I've driven up this road. I didn't intend to be away for that long, but life just sort of *happened*.

It feels like the journey up the driveway takes almost as long as the drive from the airport. Deep puddles and mud holes slow us to a crawl. The clouds darken the night, making the headlights of the taxi the only source of light as we near the old farm where I was raised by my grandparents. The house is in darkness, except for a faint glow I see in the kitchen window. I blink quickly, certain that the light is playing tricks on my eyes because I think I see my nana standing there. She passed away more than ten years ago, but I'd like to believe her spirit is still around. Especially now.

I pay the driver and express my disgust at the fare. Since buses or trains only run this far north of the city during rush hour, I really had no other choice. I get out of the car and stare at the desolate house. I hear the cab's trunk unlatch, but I suppose the driver has no intention of helping me with my luggage since he doesn't move from his seat. I wish I'd withheld his tip until he helped me to the door.

It's eerily quiet tonight, except for the rumbling of thunder in the distance. As I watch the tail lights of the cab disappear at the end of the driveway, I feel alone. I'd give anything to hear those old familiar country sounds right now; the frogs or the crickets. I think I'd even find the howling of coyotes soothing at the moment.

The porch light comes on as I drag the heavy trunk through the mud to the overgrown pathway. The house looks odd without the roof covering the porch. Pops had told me the old rotten wood didn't withstand the weight of all the snow last winter and collapsed. I wonder why he didn't replace it, since he worked hard to buy this house before he asked Nana to marry him and had always taken great pride in it.

I must be holding my breath, because I'm starting to feel a little light-headed. I've never wanted to look up and see my pops standing on the porch, more than I do right now. My heart sinks as I pull fifty pounds of clothing up the porch steps and accept the fact the light, which has illuminated my way to the front door, is on a sensor. There's nobody waiting for me here.

I dig through the dirt of an old flowerpot, where the spare key was always hidden, and come up empty. Awesome, what next? I obviously just jinxed myself because the sky opens up and dumps a fury of rain right over my head while I root around in the darkness searching for the key. Unsuccessful, I stand in the doorway, using the screen door to shelter me from the downpour. The wind changes direction and I lean back against the front door and take a deep breath, trying to avoid getting drenched.

Suddenly and unexpectedly the door flies open, and I stumble backward, before losing my balance and hitting the floor with a loud, squishy thud. I look up at the unfamiliar aluminum front door and wonder what happened to the sturdy solid oak door that was here for almost seventy years. Getting to my feet, I shiver from the cold damp air as I reach for the light switch. I get a good look around the dusty room before the storm makes the light flicker and the power goes out, leaving me in complete darkness.

I fight the urge to break down. My body is still on Central European Time and thinks it's five in the morning. Exhausted and feeling cold in my damp clothes, I stack some kindling and light the woodstove. The flickering light of the flames illuminates the room. I make my way to the reclining chair in the corner and grab an old, tattered blanket from a nearby stool and wrap it around me before I plop myself, wearily, into the seat. The leather is well worn and soft, and when I finally feel the warmth from the fire, I close my eyes.

In the murky place between reality and dreams I hear my own childhood laughter echoing in the distance. As I'm whisked deeper through the vortex of REM sleep, muffled voices become clearer. Suddenly, I'm a five-year-old girl again, wearing rubber boots and standing nearly knee-deep in the back pond trying to catch tadpoles.

"Nana is going to skin you alive if you track any of that mud into the house."

"I won't," I promise, as I take another step and sink farther into the mud. The pond water rushes over the edge of the rubber and into my boots.

Pops chuckles at the face I make as I try to move my heavy feet, in pond water-filled rubbers, toward him. "Guess there was no point in putting them on," he muses.

When I lift my leg to step onto the shore, my boot stays stuck in the clay. I try to balance on one foot while I find my footing in the dry grass. As I begin to tip backward, Pops reaches out and tries to get a hold of me, but he's not fast enough, and I land on my bottom, in the shallow water.

A huge bullfrog jumps from a nearby lily pad and lands on my chest. My eyes widen as he begins to croak angrily, as if he's telling me a thing or two about pond life etiquette, before launching himself into the cloudy water.

I look up at Pops and raise a curious brow. "What the hell was he complaining about? I'm the one with wet knickers," I announce innocently. He starts to laugh. One of those real hard belly laughs; the contagious kind. It makes me start to giggle. He steps into the water and reaching down with strong hands, he gets a grip on me, pulls me out of the water, and puts me onto the grass.

I pick up my bucket and look disappointed. Pop tousles my hair. "Maybe next time you'll catch some tadpoles."

He dumps the water out of my boots and steadies them so I can put them back on. "Did my momma like to catch tadpoles?" I ask curiously.

I reach up and hold his hand as we walk back to the house.

"Nope. Your momma didn't like to do outdoor stuff. She was all about finger painting and drawing pictures."

I wrinkle my nose and make him chuckle again. "That sounds boring."

As we exit the heavily wooded land into the meadow, the sun becomes almost blinding. Pops takes off his old worn-out baseball cap and plops it on my head. I look up at him, squinting from beneath the brim. "Sometimes, I forget what her face looks like, so I sneak into Nana's chest and look at the pictures she hides in there."

He peers down at me. "You best not let her catch you."

"Why does she hide them?"

He pauses a moment, looking rather sad. "I suppose seeing them makes her miss your momma too."

"Is that why she cries sometimes?"

Pop just keeps on walking. "Sometimes. Sometimes women cry and nobody knows why."

He looks down to see my concerned look as I struggle to keep up with him. "I'll ask Nana to pick out her favourite picture of your momma and give it to you. That way you'll always have a memory of her face."

My smile grows wide. "Thank you, Pops."

"Mmmhmm."

"My clothes are almost dry, so maybe she won't be aggravated with me for falling in the pond again."

He grins. "That's an awfully big word for a five-year-old."

"I like words. When I'm bigger I'm going to know every word in the world."

"Well, best you don't ever be saying that H-word around your nana, little girl."

I'm only five, but I know exactly which word he's referring to. I give him an amused grin. "You say it all the time."

He stops and crouches down to my level. "How about **you** don't say it and keep us both out of trouble?"

I think on it a moment. "If I promise not to say it anymore, will you let me drive the tractor?"

He raises his brows.

"I want to steer by myself. And go faster."

Pops scratches his head and laughs once aloud. "Deal. But we won't tell Nana about that either."

I open my eyes at sunrise still sitting in the chair, fully dressed. I think there's something about the country that syncs to one's soul. It's as if I never left. I get to my feet and stretch, looking around the room which is beginning to brighten up with the rising sun. Not much has changed, it's just a little bit dustier. But then, Pops had never been much of a housekeeper.

I drag my trunk up the stairs to my old room, hesitating as I pass my momma's door. I'm tempted to peek in, but I need to get out of these clothes and have a hot shower. I groan as I turn the shower knob and no water comes out. How could I have forgotten that no power means no well pump for water either?

I might as well get some chores out of the way before I go into town to meet with the funeral home. I struggle to lift the trunk up on the bed and rummage through the designer clothes I brought with me. They're really no use here, but all I own now is office attire; there's no time for recreation in my life in France. I throw on some of Pops' old work clothes and make my way out to the chicken coop.

After Nana died, Pops lost interest in almost everything to do with farming. He stopped planting crops, leased the land to other farmers, and sold off all the animals except for the chickens. Even when money was tight, he could never bring himself to sell the eggs. We kept what we needed for ourselves and traded neighbours for things like honey and fresh vegetables. He claimed that he was getting too old and tired to keep up with the work, but I suspect he just missed her.

Thank the Lord the storm has passed. It's going to take days for things to dry up. I tread through the soaked boggy grass toward the coop. Just inside the door, the metal bucket is still hanging on a rusty old nail. "Okay, girls," I announce, as I take the bucket from the wall. "The old sheriff is back in town." I turn and stop in my tracks, completely stunned to find it vacant. Not one chicken, not one cluck, no eggs or chicks. Nada. Nothing. My heart starts to race, and I can't breathe. I fly out the door, gasping for air and hoping for relief from my panic attack as I head back to the house and sit on the porch step. "What in the *hell* was going on around here while I was away?" I wonder aloud. I raise my eyes to the sky. "Sorry, Nana."

CHAPTER TWO

I look at the time on my phone and realize I need to get ready to go into town. I lay out one of my favourite business outfits on the bed, then plug the bathroom sink and dump what's left of my water bottle into it. A quick wash will have to do for now. Before I leave, I give myself an extra squirt of my expensive perfume, hoping nobody will know I haven't had a proper shower.

I grab the key ring from the rack beside the front door and make my way to the old barn where Pops used to store the vehicles. He kept up the license and paid the insurance on my old car for when I came to visit. I supposed that was several years of money wasted. The guilt starts to weigh on me as I push on the rusty old barn door hinges with everything I have. Beneath the streams of sunlight, let in by the holes in the roof, sits the first car I ever owned, covered in an inch of dust. She was already ten years old when I bought her with the money I made working after school at the small-town coffee shop.

It takes a few turns of the key, but the old car eventually comes to life. It's apparent from the bouncing and squeaking as I travel down the driveway that she's in bad need of new shocks or something. Note to self; add *sell the car* to the list of things I need to deal with in the week I've taken as vacation from my job.

I can barely see through the front window from all the dust. I turn on the wipers and curse when they smear the dirt, making it worse. The old girl starts to sputter so I give her some gas to keep her from stalling, but the end of the driveway comes up sooner than I was expecting, and I have to hit the brakes hard. Panic washes over me as the pedal sinks to the floor and I realize I'm not going to stop. Pumping the brakes frantically, I pray for it to restore some pressure as I fly out the end of the driveway and onto the muddy dirt road. I crank the wheel hard, hoping the gravel will slow me down.

A driver in a pickup truck leans on the horn and hits the brakes, trying to avoid me. I no longer have any control of my car as I slide and fishtail all over the road, eventually coming to a complete stop, facing backward in the ditch.

The driver of the truck gets out, wanders over to the edge of the ditch, and looks down at me. I must be a little dazed, because he's talking to me, but all I hear is garbled sounds as I stare at him through the dirt-smeared front window. As my adrenaline slows down, and the sound of blood rushing through my brain begins to fade, I find the sense to roll down the side window so I can hear him.

"Are you hurt?"

"No, I'm just a little...terrified."

I'm blinded by the bright sun behind him and try to block it with my hand. "The brakes went out."

I hear a loud clashing of metal and try to look through the mud splatters on the front windshield as the passenger of the truck, wearing blue jeans and a baseball cap, tries to hook a chain to the undercarriage of my car. After some cursing, he abandons his efforts and tosses the chain back into the bed of the truck with a crash.

"You might want to get out of the car," the guy on the shoulder of the road says, irritably. He takes a few steps closer and blocks the sun, revealing his sandy brown hair and serious disposition. Now I can see who I'm dealing with.

I look out the window at the foot of storm water I'm parked in and growl as I hold my forehead. "I just don't want to deal with this day."

I procrastinate, staring at the breadth of his shoulders and masculine lines. With his phone to his ear, he looks down at me impatiently. "What are you waiting for? Are you afraid you'll melt if you get wet?"

"No. I...I..." Apparently stuttering is my new response to stress. I don't like it. Take a breath. Get a grip. "I'm on my way to the funeral home to make arrangements for my pops. I'm going to be late."

He glances at the driveway I just shot out of and then over at the other man. As I'm about to get out, he shoves his phone back into his pocket and hollers. "Hold on! There's something jammed against the door."

The mountain of muscle in blue denim slides down the side of the ditch, into the foot of cold water, and makes his way to the car. He pulls and kicks at a large log wedged against the bottom of the door panel. Unsuccessful, he stands and wipes the dirt off his forehead with the back of his hand. When he leans down to talk to me through the window, I get my first good look at his brilliant blue eyes. A well-trimmed beard frames his ruggedly handsome, mud-streaked face.

"What's your name?" he asks.

I don't answer. I'm too busy looking at the dark tribal tattoos on his forearms.

"Miss? Did you hit your head? Do you know your name?"

"Cora. Sorry, my name is Cora Scott."

He pauses, and his jaw tightens. "I'm Ben, that's my younger brother, Jake." The taller, clean-shaven young man waves when I look up. "Let's get you out of here and on your way," Ben continues.

"How?"

"Out the window."

Is he out of his mind? "Out the window?" I confirm.

"Yeah, out the window. You set out the open window and I'll pick you up and carry you to dry land."

"Oh!" I say nervously. "I don't think that's a good idea."

"Do you want to get about your business today or are you gonna swim there?"

I curse, and it makes Jake chuckle.

"Let's go," Ben prompts, tapping on the door ledge. Jake turns the truck around and pulls over to the side of the road.

I undo my seat belt and then grab my wallet and cell phone. "I can't believe I'm doing this."

"If you're gonna live out here, you best get a pickup truck...or learn how to drive."

What is this guy's deal? I flash him an unimpressed look before I wriggle myself into position, halfway in and halfway out the window. Ben tucks his arms beneath me and lifts me like I weigh no more than a ten-pound bag of potatoes.

I squeal.

He looks at me startled. "Don't worry, I won't put you down and ruin your fancy shoes." The water makes a swishing sound as he makes his way, in heavy boots, up the side of the ditch toward his waiting brother. Jake opens the driver's door of the Chevy and Ben lifts me in and sets me on the seat.

"What's going on?" I ask, confused.

"You're going to take my truck into town."

"What about my car?" I ask concerned.

"See that tractor coming down the road?"

I lean out the window. "Yes."

"That's our father. I called him a few minutes ago so we can tow your car back up to your house."

"How will I get your truck back to you after?"

"We'll come around and collect it. Don't worry. Just go and tend to your family business."

I'm humbled by his kindness. "You don't even know me."

"This is Mono Mills," Jake says through the open window. "You're a neighbour. Around here, we help each other out."

He gives me a sweet reassuring smile and for the first time in days, I feel the sun shining on me. "Thank you."

Ben wanders to the front of the truck and bangs on the hood. "You best get on your way. Better part of the day is gone, and we've got a lot of work to do today. Your little off-road adventure put us behind an hour."

"What's with him and banging on things?"

Jake gives me an apologetic smile. "Drive safe, and I'm sorry for your loss."

I glance into the rearview mirror and catch Ben watching as I drive away. I wonder why he's so uptight. His brother seems nice. I turn on the radio to distract my thoughts and get lost in the soothing sound of music. Sometimes in France, when I'm feeling homesick, I'll find a country music station on the satellite radio and put on my headphones because it draws some very odd looks from the European crowd.

It doesn't take me long to drive into town at all. The good thing about a small-town funeral parlour is they treat everyone like family. Now Pops is gone, it's scary to think I have no family left; unless his sister is still alive. The last I heard about Aunt Bea was that she was too stubborn to sell her house and move into a retirement home, so she hired some help and stayed put. Pops said he felt sorry for the person who had to deal with her. She was a firecracker, even when she was in the best of moods.

I've been to a few funerals in my life, but I've never had to plan one. Nana's was a quiet, private family thing that Pops and Aunt Bea looked after.

A well-dressed young man welcomes me and opens the door. Despite the effort, and extensive design budget, the place gives me the wiggins. As I enter the office, where I'll make the final arrangements, I feel like I'm living some weird movie scene mash-up between *Weekend At Bernie's* and *The Hills Have Eyes.*

I sit at the desk and wait out a long awkward pause where I assume the funeral director is going to give me some direction. "I have no idea where to start or what to do," I finally begin.

He nods and picks up a file folder that has my pops name labeled on the tab. "It looks like your grandfather came to see us a few years ago to make arrangements."

I raise my brow in curiosity. "That's a big relief. I have no idea what his wishes were. We never talked about it."

"That's not uncommon," he assures me, as he reads the document in front of him.

"I don't even know what kind of casket to buy."

"You won't need to buy a casket."

My mind strays back to my earlier thoughts, and I envision myself walking in to the room to find my embalmed Pops posed in the chair in the parlour, handing out cigars and cartons of eggs to those who drop in to say goodbye. I give my head a shake. Dear Lord, what is wrong with me? I tune back in to the details.

"Your grandfather has arranged one visitation day for friends and family, after which he wishes to be cremated."

It takes me a moment to process that, and I back the conversation up. "I'm sorry, but why isn't he being buried beside Nana?"

"Apparently, he sold the adjoining plot."

"Oh. I wasn't aware of that." When my mother died, they laid her to rest in the old church cemetery on the Seventh Line and Pops bought the last three plots remaining for Nana, himself and his younger sister, so they'd all be together. It seems odd to me that he didn't tell me that he sold it.

"He asked us to make arrangements to have his ashes buried with your grandmother in her plot, but there are additional charges for that."

"Well, at least they'll be together. How much will that cost?"

"That brings me to my next point. I'm afraid that I have to inform you of this, but it appears he stopped making payments and there's a balance that will need to be paid."

I start to get that feeling of guilt again. "I've been out of the country for a few years. There's a lot of things he didn't tell me." He passes me a copy of the statement and balance due. "Whoa! Does this have to be paid before the funeral?"

"No. We can make payment arrangements for the balance and anything else you'd like to add."

"Add? I don't know how I'm going to pay for this."

"Well, the government does provide a small financial reimbursement toward it, but the balance is most often paid by surviving family members or from the funds of the estate."

I must look really confused right now. "Have you met with his lawyer about the will and settling the estate?" he asks.

"Err. No. I don't even know who his lawyer is."

"I'm sure there's a will somewhere. He seems like the kind who would have all his legal ducks in a row. You just need to find them."

I suppose this numb feeling I'm experiencing is a defense mechanism kicking in to help me get through this conversation. I leave there feeling like I've just gone several rounds in an MMA battle of emotions. There's no dainty way to climb up into this massive truck, but I do my best, trying to avoid getting covered in mud. As I drive through town, my mind begins to become preoccupied with all the questions I need answered.

A loud obnoxious horn startles me, and I realize I've been sitting at a green light. I give the guy behind me an apologetic wave and roll through the intersection as the light turns to yellow. I can hear cursing from the vehicle behind me. I'm not sure why, but I don't want to drive through town. I make a sharp right and head toward one of the old concession roads that will lead me to the north and away from the traffic and people.

As I reach the end of the paved road and hit the dirt and gravel, I roll down the windows and turn up the music. Tears fill my eyes, and I unsuccessfully try to blink them away as I pull into the driveway and spot a pair of legs sticking out from underneath my car. I'm not sure if it's the sound of the big V8 engine or the vibration of the excessive music volume that announces my arrival, but he slides out and gets to his feet.

Damn. I wasn't expecting him to be here. He lowers the jack and rolls it back into the garage, then wipes the grease off his hands with an old rag. I can't take my eyes off of him. Stroking his beard, he walks toward the truck and opens the door. I try to hide it, but he can tell I've been crying. As I swing myself sideways, he grabs my waist with his strong hands and slowly lowers me to the ground. I ignore my body's reaction when my hands glide down his rock-hard chest until my feet touch the ground. It takes a moment to gather my thoughts. "Ben, right?" I ask for clarification.

"Right."

"What are you doing with my car?" I ask softly, trying to focus myself on something besides the tingles that just ran through me.

"Looking at the brakes."

I furrow my brow. "You don't need to do that."

"Well, we can't have you taking out all the neighbours on the road until you decide to get them looked after. Some of us need our vehicles to get to work."

"Now wait a minute," I say defensively. "I wasn't putting off having them fixed. I haven't been home in a few years. The car has been sitting for a long time."

"Even more reason not to drive the damn thing until you had it checked out."

My blood boils! "I'll have it towed somewhere tomorrow and have it looked at."

"No need." He steps onto the running board and slides into the driver seat. I jump as he slams the door. "The brakes are fixed." He puts the truck in reverse and leans out the open window. "And I changed the oil."

I glance over at the car. I can't figure out if he's an asshole or a good guy. I turn to thank him but he's already pulling away. "Wait!" I call out. "How much do I owe you?"

"Nothing," he hollers out the window. "Just look after your vehicle maintenance from now on."

My shoulders fall. He's definitely an asshole.

CHAPTER THREE

I watch as he disappears into the horizon. I don't know if it's because I want to make sure he leaves, or if I'm stalling because I don't want to go into the house. At least the power is back on. It takes forever for the hot water to get upstairs to the second-floor shower, but it feels heavenly once it does. I stand under the water for a long time, after I finish washing the shampoo out of my hair. It isn't until a large air pocket interrupts the flow of water and makes a blood-curdling vibration throughout the pipes, that I decide to get out and dry off.

I've got a lot of things to figure out in the next few days. I guess it's a good thing I haven't had much of an appetite, since there's not a lick of food in this house. I repeatedly open cupboard doors, looking for a can of soup or anything that might help keep my energy up. I hear a vehicle on the gravel road and watch out the window as an approaching car appears. When the elderly woman parks in front of the house and gets out, I'm already standing at the bottom of the porch steps.

She smiles. "Hello, dear. You must be Cora."

"I am."

"Oh, that's lovely. I'm Nancy, from the church," she clarifies. "It was my turn to cook." She holds out a plastic container. "Bill must be so happy you've come to visit. I've brought my famous meatloaf. It's his favourite. I'm sure there's enough for both of you."

I smile apologetically. "I'm afraid my grandfather has passed away."

"I'm sorry, dear. I didn't know."

"That's okay," I assure her. "I'm sorry you came all the way out here for no reason."

"Nonsense, you look like you haven't had a half decent meal in a long time. You take it." She hands me the container and I have to admit it smells delicious.

"You can't live on croissants and red wine, you know."

I laugh as I walk her back to her car. "Ah, Pops has been talking about me."

"We enjoyed each other's company sometimes. He loved you more than anything."

I nod and fight back the tears.

"Sorry for your loss, dear. I guess the good Lord knows best. Bill was in a bad way for quite some time. That's no way to be living."

My eyes open wide. "Excuse me?" I say dumbfounded. "He was sick for a long time?"

"Yes, with the cancer."

Every muscle in my body tightens and cramps up. I feel like I've just been punched in the stomach. "I had no idea he was diagnosed with cancer."

She purses her lips, and there is sadness in her eyes. I can tell she regrets being the one to tell me. "About a year ago. He decided against chemo treatments since he didn't want to prolong a life of pain. I think he was just ready to be with Maggie again."

I wave as she pulls away and then walk back to the house feeling heavy-hearted. I can't believe what I just heard. I talked to Pops a few weeks back, and he sounded tired and a little lonely, but he neglected to mention he was dying of cancer. That's something you'd mention to your family, right? When I asked the hospital how he died, they said that his heart stopped, and it was his time to go.

I devour Nancy's meatloaf, while I sort through papers I found in the desk, and I can see why it's *famous*. Midway through the stack, I find what I'm looking for, in a thick unopened package from Gordon Henderson Legal Services. I use my dinner knife to open the envelope, smearing the documents inside with gravy. I inhale slowly as I slide it out and view the words; *last will and testament*.

Panic washes over me. I can't do this. I don't *want* to do this. I stuff it back into the envelope and walk away, hoping if I pretend the document doesn't exist my pops will come back to life. My phone rings and I glance down at the number. "Hello."

"Bonjour, Cheri. Are you okay? You didn't call to let me know you arrived safely."

"Etienne, I'm sorry. I just have so much going on in my brain right now."

"I understand. I just wanted to make sure that you're all right."

"All right?" A moment of distress finally catches up with me. "No! I'm not all right. The man who was a father to me, my entire life, is gone. Nothing here is the same, and I have no clue what I'm supposed to be doing."

"Yes, of course, you're upset. It's a very sad time."

I close my eyes and sigh. "I'm sorry. I'm just really stressed out."

"When you come home to France, we'll go out for a nice dinner and talk. I'm here for you."

It doesn't feel like it or he'd be here with me right now. We've been casually dating for a little over a year now, and he says he wants to take things to the next level and move in together. I like him, but for some reason, I'm hesitant. "That sounds nice. Thank you. I have to see the lawyer and figure out what has to be done as far as settling the estate and income taxes and all that."

"When is the funeral?"

"The day after tomorrow. I know it's probably too late to book a flight, but do you think you could get here?"

"Cora, you know I can't leave work. They'd be suspicious."

"Oh, of course. I totally understand," I mask my disappointment, even though I'm sure it has nothing to do with anyone finding out about our relationship. There was a huge opportunity at work to take on a campaign for one of our largest clients, and Etienne chose to stay in France and apply for the position. I would have welcomed that opportunity, but I had no choice but to come home. "I should get going. I have a lot to do."

"Of course. Je t'aime."

I hesitate. "Me too." It's all I can manage right now.

I call the lawyer first thing in the morning and the secretary tells me to come straight in. I cautiously drive my car into town, unsure of what other mechanical failures await me. I noticed the sign out front of the century-old home that houses Gordon Henderson Legal Services yesterday, so I know exactly where I'm going.

The woman at the front desk extends her condolences. As she walks me into an office at the back of the hallway, I run my hand along the polished bannister.

"It's beautiful."

She gives me a polite smile. "We've spent the last two years having this building restored."

"That seems like a long time," I say as I seat myself.

"Yeah, well we hired a local restoration specialist. He's an extremely annoying perfectionist." She straightens a pile of papers on the desk. "But nice to look at," she adds. "They packed up all their things a few days ago. It's glorious not to be dealing with the power tools and the pounding and the sawdust."

"I bet."

A rather lanky man rushes into the room and grabs a folder from the top of the file. The woman nods at me and exits, pulling the door closed. I begin to wonder if he even knows I'm in the room. Several minutes pass before he looks up and acknowledges me.

"Miss Scott."

"Yes," I confirm.

"Gordon Henderson. I'm sorry for your loss. Bill was a great man."

"Did you know my grandfather well?"

"Yes, we both attended the men's breakfasts at the church."

I'm thankful for the fellowship and friendship the parishioners from my grandfather's church provided him in my absence.

He sits back in his chair, pursing his lips. "Cora, you're named as the executor and sole beneficiary."

"What does that mean?"

"Simply put, the entire estate has been left to you."

"There's an estate?"

He nods politely and explains. "The land and vehicles are assets, along with any livestock or farm equipment. You'll be responsible for settling the outstanding debts and filing the final taxes."

My eyes open wide. "How much debt?"

He leans forward and picks up the file in front of him and rubs his chin. "A sizeable amount, at last check." He scribbles something down on a piece of paper and slides it across the table to me. "Don't worry about any of this now. Say goodbye to your grandfather tomorrow and give yourself a day to breathe. This is the name of one of our acquaintances who's an accountant. She'll help you figure it out."

"Thank you." An overwhelming rush of emotions stalls me. I fold the paper in half, then in half again and again.

The chair legs make a creaking sound on the floor as Gordon gets to his feet. "Come see me in a few days, and we'll get started on tying up all the loose ends."

I force myself to look up and nod. That numb feeling creeps over me again as I walk toward the front door. Is this all my grandfather's life amounted to? Debt and loose ends?

I stand outside the house, remembering how it looked when I was growing up here. It was always immaculate, from the walkway that led to the front door to the peaks on the second-floor roof. There was always a fresh coat of white paint on the pillars that held up the tin roof over the porch. Nana loved to sit out there in the evenings, so she always kept it swept clean. She would watch from the kitchen window and yell at us to take off our muddy boots at the bottom of the steps. Now the paint is bubbled and peeling, and the glass windows surrounding what used to be a solid oak door are covered in dust and cobwebs. Fall leaves have blown into the corners and piled up there. The eavestroughs are rusty and coming apart at the joints, where it appears birds have been nesting. New life sprouts up in the overgrown flower garden. From one end of the porch to the other, there was a time no weed would dare take root here.

Something draws my attention to the second-floor window, and I study it intensely until I become cold and weary and go inside. I can't put it off any longer. It's time to start packing things up. I walk up the narrow stairway and push open the door to my grandparents' room and go straight to the chest at the end of the bed. While I'm searching for the key, I come across a stack of photo albums in the corner. I take them back to my room and sit on the bed, turning pages for hours and cherishing every photo of my mother and me together. "I wish I could have known you better."

CHAPTER four

I'm relieved to find Pops isn't propped up in a chair in the parlour when I arrive at the funeral home. I guess it's the twisted way my mind deals with uncomfortable situations.

I slowly walk toward the casket, hesitating a few times. Suddenly, I'm not a confident, successful thirty-one-year-old woman. I'm a terrified little girl, who's lost the only father she's ever known. There won't be any more lazy Sunday afternoons fishing by the pond. No more tractor pulls that we didn't tell Nana about. Christmas, Thanksgiving, Easter...every happy childhood memory I have comes back to me in a few fleeting moments. I'm on the verge of hyperventilating when a woman walks over to where I've stopped in the middle of the room.

"It's okay, if you'd like to wait for the rest of the family."

I stare at the large wooden casket and swallow hard. "There's only me." I feel a twitch in my chin, and I try to get control of my faculties before my bottom lip starts to tremble.

She gives me a sympathetic smile. "Take all the time you need."

I finally find the strength to walk the rest of the way to the open coffin and stare down at him. This is not how I remember him. It's not how I *want* to remember him. He looks...frail...fragile. He looks *old*. This is not my pops. My pops was strong and handsome. He could split a bush cord of wood in an afternoon with nothing but an axe. He could bale hay for sixteen hours straight, then go home and tend to the chores and do it all again the following day. Trembling, I reach out to touch him, but his cold, rigid hand offers me no comfort.

Tears stream down my cheeks, and I force myself to take a breath, as the funeral director stands at my side offering me a tissue. As I dab the moisture from my eyes she quietly whispers, "People are beginning to arrive for the visitation. We'll have them wait in the other room until you're ready."

I wipe my nose, grab a few more tissues from the box, and stuff them into my pocket.

"What am I supposed to do?"

"It's up to you. Most people choose to stand at the front of the room, so visitors can convey their condolences after they've said goodbye."

"Okay, I'm ready. Let them in." I don't think I could feel more alone than I do now. I wish Etienne was here. His only contribution toward being comforting was the bottle of anti-anxiety pills he slipped into my hand when we said goodbye. I took one of those in the parking lot when I got here a half an hour ago, and I'm pretty sure it's already starting to kick in.

There's a constant line of people through the room. Most of whom I've never met before. Dear sweet Nancy arrives and is kind enough to introduce me to her fellow church parishioners. At least for a few moments I feel like there's someone in the room I know. My body aches, after being on my feet for hours, and I have no idea when I ate last. Everything and everyone has been a blur.

I reach out to shake the hand of the next man in line and feel a little confused because he looks familiar. I realize why as I recognize the man standing beside him. Judging from the resemblance they are certainly related.

"Cora," Jake says warm-heartedly. "I don't think you actually met my father the other day. We sent you on your way into town, while he pulled your car out of the ditch with his tractor."

"Phil," the old man says still holding onto my hand.

"Thank you for rescuing me."

"Just being neighbourly. Your grandfather used to help me work on that old tractor."

I manage a small smile. "There wasn't much my pops couldn't do."

"He'll be missed."

Jake gently nudges him along. "We can visit later, Dad. There are a lot of people waiting."

"We're just a few farms over," Phil reminds me before he moves along.

Jake reaches out and touches my arm. "If there's anything you need, let us know." He steps to the side, leaving me face-to-face with his brother. Contrary to his previously hard disposition, today Ben greets me with a sympathetic and kind smile. A strange, distraught feeling begins to break through the haze induced by the pills. I reach for the outstretched hand in front of me, and when my eyes lock to his, the emotional floodgates burst open, and I break down into a hard sob. His strong arms surround me, pull me to his chest, and hold me firmly. As I take a few stuttered breaths and try to compose myself, I realize I've found comfort in the arms of a perfect stranger. Embarrassed, I pull away and apologize.

"It's okay," Ben assures me. "Maybe you need to take a little break."

"Can I do that?" I ask sniffling.

"We can do that," he assures me, turning to the room. "Ladies and gentlemen," he begins. "Thank you for coming. Cora needs to take a short break. If you'd like to offer your condolences, please help yourself to a coffee and a sandwich and she'll be back in ten minutes or so." He keeps a gentle hold of my elbow and guides me through the room.

"There's sandwiches?"

"Yes."

I lean in, trying to be inconspicuous. "How are there sandwiches?" I ask confused.

"Usually Miss Nancy and the church group." He stops and studies me. "When was the last time you ate?"

I shrug, and he expresses his discontent. "You have to look after your body the same as a vehicle. You need the proper fuel." He clenches his jaw and lets out a small growl. "Look who I'm talking to. I've seen how you look after your car."

He hands me an egg salad sandwich and I don't dare refuse it.

"Do you need a drink?"

"Make it a double," I joke.

He scowls at me. "Your choices are juice or water. And you really shouldn't drink alcohol with the pills you've taken."

I feel my jaw drop. How did he know? "Water, please."

By the time he returns, I've completely devoured the egg salad and I'm halfway through my second ham and pickle sandwich.

"Feeling better?" he asks, genuinely concerned.

"Yes. Thank you." My face turns red. "I'm really sorry about that." I feel so awkward. "In there. You know; losing it on you."

"There's no shame in showing your sorrow."

"Still, I hope I didn't make you feel uncomfortable."

"Why would that make me feel uncomfortable?"

"You just don't seem like that kind of guy."

He raises a brow. "I don't seem like a caring and sensitive kind of guy?"

Crap. Now I've done it. "I'm sorry, I didn't mean that..."

He half grins and interrupts my rambling, "No, you're right. Jake's the nice one. I'm the hard-ass."

I decide against agreeing with him. "I think I'm okay to go back now."

He nods, then takes the water bottle out of my hand and puts it down on the table. I'm very aware of his hand on my back as he gently escorts me back.

There's been a change in atmosphere in the room since we left. The overwhelming tension has finally lifted. The long line at the casket has dispersed, and people have gathered into small groups to chat while they wait for the service. Jake has taken over as host and deals with anything that comes up. His father, Phil, introduces me to all the old friends and neighbours that I've long since forgotten. Nancy and the women's church auxiliary group rush around, making sure everyone has had their fill of sandwiches and baked goods. And Ben? Well, he stands out of the way and observes, ready to act if needed. Every time I glance his way, he's staring at me. I find it oddly comforting. I can still smell his cologne from when I was firmly pressed against his rock-hard chest. I thought he was handsome in his jeans, but I'm not going to lie, he wears a suit and tie well.

The remaining hour seems to fly by quickly. People begin to wander into the chapel for the final service. Jake checks with me to see if there's anything I need before we head in. "I didn't know funerals could be so hectic," I say wearily.

"Your pops was well known in all the counties in the Hills of the Headwaters."

"Well, I'm glad he was blessed with so many friends while I was halfway around the world..." I pause, choking back the emotions.

"Don't," Jake interrupts. "Don't do that to yourself."

I nod, then someone catches my eye. "Aunt Bea!" I gasp at the sight of the elderly woman making her way across the room with assistance. She's still alive! Just barely, apparently. I hope I didn't say that out loud.

I wait until after she's had time say goodbye to Pops, then nod at the staff to proceed with the closing of the casket.

I place my hand on her back, as I join her. "Aunt Bea. Do you remember me?"

"Eh?" she says loudly.

"Do you remember me? I'm Cora," I repeat louder.

"Of course, I remember you! I'm deaf, not senile."

I try not to laugh, but it isn't easy when I glance over her shoulder to see Ben smiling. "Would you please sit with me during the service?"

"That would be nice, yes."

I haven't seen the woman in nearly fifteen years, but it's comforting to not be sitting alone. When a moment in the service brings my emotions to the surface again, a large firm hand squeezes my shoulder from behind. I don't have to turn to know it's Ben.

When the minister is finished with his service, he invites people to the front of the room. As members of Pops' church and agricultural club share their stories of him, it becomes even more clear that Pop had been sick for some time, and I was the only one who didn't know. I look down at the piece of paper I've been holding tightly in my fidgeting hands and realize the speech I was going to give isn't appropriate. It makes me feel sick inside, to know he was here suffering while I was in Europe chasing a career. Deep down, I know that's exactly the reason he didn't tell me.

When it appears everyone who wants to speak has had their turn, I get to my feet and take a breath as I approach the podium. I fold the paper and stuff it into my pocket. Hands shaking, I look up as I address the room.

I feel my face turn red. "Wow," I say softly, feeling overwhelmed. "It's hard to know where to start." I glance over at Ben and he gives me a reassuring nod. "William and Margaret Scott were my *grandparents*. They raised me in the absence of my birth parents, and I hope I made them feel they did so without regret." I take a quick sip of water to quench my dry mouth.

"I had a wonderful childhood full of laughter and joyful memories. That's who Margaret and William were. Maggie and Bill; kind, loving people. After my nana passed away, I could see, at times, my grandfather struggled to find a reason to live without her." I lower my eyes a moment to compose myself. "But he was a stubborn, strong man, as most of you know. Even when things got tough, he refused to fail. As a child, I had no idea how rough the life of a farmer is. The constant care of the land, the livestock... the people who depend on you. Pops balanced a razor-thin budget with little profit and raised a teenage girl on his own." I look around the room at the nods and acknowledgements. I shrug. "Strangely enough, I didn't know we were poor. I never felt like I was missing out on anything. Pops knew how to provide everything we needed. And he knew how to *love*. Let's face it, that's the important thing." I survey the room. "Bill Scott was never a poor man. His bank account reflected only a monetary value. In fact, Pops was rich. He measured his wealth by his friends, his family, his faith, and the love he had for all of us. He lived his life making sure that we..." I point around the room, "were all well looked after. He never wanted anything for himself, not even after the loss of his beloved Maggie. It's obvious from your kind words that Pops truly was a respected and well-loved member of the community."

I pause, watching a few elders wipe at their tears. "My pops didn't tell me he was dying. I think most of you know why that was. Like I said, he was a stubborn man." I smile at the nods around the room. "If I could change anything, I would go back in time with the knowledge I have now, and I'd come home to care for him, the way he would have cared for any of us, if the tables were turned. Cancer is an unforgiving, relentless disease, and I would have been here for him, every step of the way." I pause to wipe my tears. "But I can't turn back time, so I'd like to thank each and every one of you who looked after him for me. For those of you who took him to appointments and brought him meals; thank you. For those of you who sat with him and provided him companionship and helped him find comfort in his faith; thank you. For being there when he needed you the most, even though he would never ask for help; thank you. Most importantly, for reminding me today, my grandfather's life measured up to so much more than a broken-down farm and a pile of unpaid bills...thank you. Pops had a good life. It was a happy life. It was a *rich* life."

As I make my way back to the front row bench, I can't stop the flow of tears. Ben gets to his feet to bring me a tissue and stays with me. I sit and pull myself together, while I wait for the room to empty.

Jake places his hand on my shoulder. "I'll check with the staff to see if there's anything you need to do before you go home and rest."

"Where'd Aunt Bea go?" I ask, noticing she's no longer sitting beside me.

"She couldn't be far away," Ben says with a smirk.

I catch a glimpse of her in the foyer and I rush to catch up.

"Aunt Bea! I was wondering if you could come by the farm for lunch, before I leave. There might be something there of sentimental value that you'd like to have."

She keeps pushing her walker as she shuffles her feet toward the door, with her personal support worker close by.

"What are you serving? She's a horrible cook."

I'm stunned by her candor and scramble for a meal an elderly woman might enjoy and I won't ruin. "I could make vegetable soup and ham sandwiches, if you like."

"Ham gives me gas."

Jake and Ben chuckle and I try not to look at them.

Err. I got nothing. "Okay, something else then." I shrug. "Do you want me to pick you up?"

She stops dead. "That's what I pay *my handler* for." She points toward the support worker. "I pay her good money to do nothing but follow me around all day."

"Oh," I say, feeling embarrassed for the poor woman. "I'm sure she does a lot more than that."

She extends her hand to me. "Hi, I'm Lynn. It's okay, she doesn't mean it that way," she assures me. "I'll bring her out on Tuesday, if that's okay."

"That's great. Do you need the address?"

"No, I don't need the address," Aunt Bea barks. "Just because I'm old, you think I'd forget where my brother lived?"

"No, of course not," I say, feeling embarrassed.

She continues shuffling to the door, grumbling all the way.

The extremely patient caregiver gently rubs my arm as she passes, and gives me a sympathetic, supportive look. "She's a little out of sorts today. Don't take any of it personally."

"I'll try not to. I'm more offended for you."

She waves it off. "What you said about your grandfather in there was beautiful."

"Thank you."

I catch a glimpse of Ben standing at the door with my coat and look around the room to find it empty. I pick up my purse and take one last look at the front of the parlour. Pops is no longer there.

"They've taken him to prepare him for cremation," Ben explains.

My lip begins to tremble as Ben holds up my jacket and I turn to slip it on. His fingers brush across the nape of my neck as he untucks my hair from the collar, and I feel a moment of peace and security.

"Can I have your car keys, please?"

I turn to look at him. "Why?"

"I'm going to drive you home in your car, and Jake's gonna follow in my truck."

"That's not necessary," I insist. After all that's gone on today, I just want to be alone with my thoughts.

"Yes, it is, and I'm not taking no for an answer."

I begin to gear up for an argument, but I get to second gear and realize I just don't have the energy. The tension in my shoulders relaxes as I hand him the key, without another word.

I'm not sure if I'm annoyed or turned on by his slight victory smile. It draws my attention to the rugged cut of his jaw. I catch myself staring at his lips and feel a sudden warmth wash over me when he seems to notice. I need to get outside for some fresh air. Quick.

I get to the car, several steps ahead of him, and pull on the door handle. I wait a moment and pull it again. Any normal person would have unlocked it with the remote, but Ben makes me wait. He looks pleased with himself as he joins me at the passenger side door, unlocks it, and opens the door for me. I'm not good at hiding my frustration as I shoulder past him to get in. Jake pulls up beside us and waits, but when Ben turns the key, he receives a very unhealthy sounding groan from the engine. He tries again, pressing his foot to the floor on the gas and holding it.

"Don't pump the gas, you'll flood it," I warn.

"I know how to start a car, thanks."

Boy, he sure has a touchy ego. I sit helplessly as he attempts to get the engine to turn over. I look out the window at Jake and shrug. One final attempt has the engine wheeze out her last breath and the battery goes completely dead. I bite my lip, although I'm very tempted to comment. Ben curses and pops the hood. Jake jumps out of the truck and joins him. I'm not sure what they're looking for, but it appears to be a serious discovery of sorts. I can only imagine the conversation that will no doubt be about my horrible automotive neglect. I use the opportunity to dial Etienne's number. After ringing several times, it goes to his voicemail and I can't help but feel disappointed.

Jake jumps back in the truck and positions her in front of us. Ben attaches jumper cables to the powerful engine and gets back into my tired old car. First turn of the key fires her back to life. I hate to say it, but I'm glad they insisted on escorting me home. I don't know what I would have done if I was stuck here alone. I'm pretty sure Ben would never let me live it down if I had to call for a tow truck.

I open my eyes as we turn on to the gravel sideroad. I blink several times, trying to find the energy to keep them open. I must have slept all the way home. "Those pills really did a number on me," I say aloud, feeling a little ashamed.

"Apparently you need the rest."

I wipe my mouth with the back of my hand. "Please tell me I didn't drool."

He glances at me quickly. "No."

"Oh, that's good," I say relieved.

A mischievous grin, curls on his lips as he continues to stare straight ahead. "You farted like a drunken sailor..."

"What?" I say shocked.

"...and snore like my uncle Angus," he adds.

I'm horrified. "Oh my God."

"But you didn't drool at all," he chuckles.

I fold my arms in front of me and pout. "I can't believe you'd even mention it. It would have been polite to just pretend it didn't happen."

He turns into the long driveway and watches for Jake in his rearview mirror. "Where's the fun in that?"

When the car comes to a complete stop, I hesitate for a moment, staring at the kitchen window. There always seems to be some mysterious kind of ethereal presence watching from there. I give my head a shake and open the door as Ben walks around the hood of the car to meet me.

"Thank you. For everything today." I get out of the car and close the door.

He nods as he passes me my keys. As our hands touch, he says my name, and the sound of it causes goosebumps to form across my skin. I lock eyes with him and feel a strong magnetism, as if gravity is pulling me toward him.

"Are you going to be okay here alone tonight?" he asks with genuine concern.

"Yeah, I'll be fine."

"Cora," he persists, unconvinced.

I look past him at his brother sitting in his truck. "I'm fine, Ben. Jake's waiting for you." I pause on the porch and watch as they drive away, wondering what he would have done if I had answered, no. As tail lights fade in the distance, I'm alarmed by a very loud creaking sound. It's the kind of sound you hear when old rotten wood and rusty nails are stressed beyond their limits and they're about to unwillingly abandon their structure. My foot breaks through a board before I can move, and then with a deafening crash, I'm completely swallowed. Flat on my back, staring up at the stars, surrounded by rubble, I curse. "Just awesome."

CHAPTER FIVE

I cringe when I climb out of bed the next morning. Today is not the day I'll brave my emotions and investigate my mother's room. I stare at it as I walk past, expecting the door to fly open and startle me. I've definitely watched too many paranormal shows on TV. I check my phone for messages from Etienne and feel let down there are none. Bruised and scraped, I wander in to the kitchen to make breakfast.

I stare out the window while standing at the counter eating my toast. It's a beautiful, sunny Saturday morning and the trees that line the driveway bend in the gentle breeze. Birds land on the edge of the empty feeder, while squirrels chatter at them from above. Everybody scatters as the eight-cylinder pickup truck whips up the driveway and straight to the garage. "What the?"

I throw on a pair of sweats and a hoodie I bought at the local second-hand store in town, and twist my hair, clipping it to the top of my head in a messy bun. I look at my two hundred dollar French designer boots and then over at Pops' galoshes. They're two sizes too big, but it's an easy decision. I carefully test the footing of the old chicken feed bucket I turned upside down to use as a step outside the front door. It has no other purpose now. The constant rain has stopped, and the mud is finally drying up with the warmer air of spring. A childhood memory comes to mind as I pass the chicken coop.

Pops tells me to wait for him, but I'm eager to help with the chores. I'm strong for my age and I'm certain I don't need his help. I climb up on a bucket to reach the string that dangles from the pendant light hanging in the chicken coop. The metal bucket teeters on the rim while I stand on my tiptoes; trying to pull the string hard enough to turn on the light. I can hear the tractor coming, and I grab the shallow wicker basket from the nail on the wall. I can barely carry it empty, but I'll show Pops I can do this on my own. I gently nudge the chickens who are roosting and carefully collect the eggs and put them in the basket. I'm almost done when I hear my name.

"Cora?" Nana's voice sounds panicked. She's likely just discovered I was missing. "For heaven's sake, Bill. She's six years old. You shouldn't have taken your eyes off her," she scolds.

I look down at the full basket of eggs and beam with my accomplishment. "I'm here!" I yell as I pick up the heavy basket and push the door open with my bottom and back out. The basket is almost as tall as I am and heavy with the weight of the eggs, but I'm determined. I knock the basket with my shins with each small step I take.

"Land sakes, child!" Nana exclaims.

I stick my tongue out and grunt as I try to move the basket. May showers have left the yard a muddy mess. My boots sink in with all the extra weight, making it difficult to move my feet. I tug my leg hard to work it loose and step on a soft patch of muck. My right leg starts to slide, and I look up at my nana with wide eyes. She holds her hands out as if to steady me, but she's several feet away. Then my left leg goes, slowly slipping outward, forcing my legs apart into a very uncomfortable position. I try to pull them together, but the mud is now as slick as ice, and I stumble and slide. I drop the basket in front of me and use my arms to try and regain my balance. I look down at the contents and smile. "It's okay, Pops! None of them cracked!" I no sooner have the words out of my mouth and my feet go out from under me, and I land face first onto the basket, crushing it. I try to push myself up out of the mud, but I sink. Pops stands over me wearing his massive galoshes and grabs a hold of the seat of my pants. With one strong tug, he lifts me and carries me over to solid ground.

"I guess I cracked the eggs," I say sadly. Pop pulls a rag out of his pocket and uses it to wipe the raw egg off my face.

"I'd say so."

"Take her out to the barn and hose off all that mud and chicken poop," Nana instructs.

I look over my shoulder as Pops takes my hand and leads me to the barn. "Do you think she's mad?"

"I think she's relieved to find ya. What were you thinking?"

"I wanted to help."

"Next time, don't disappear without telling someone where you're going. You gave your Nana a scare." He turns the hose on to a gentle spray and begins to wash the filth off me. "That was a mighty ambitious chore for a squirt like you."

"I'm sorry I broke all the eggs, Pops."

He lifts me to sit on top of a bale of hay and dries off my hands and face. "Don't ever put limits on yourself, Cora. You can do anything you want to do. Never stop trying. Even if it means you break a lot of eggs until you get it right." He grabs an old milking *pail off the wall and hands it to me. "Tomorrow, you're gonna need something sturdier to collect those eggs in."*

"Good morning." I shade my eyes with my hand as I approach the barn.

"Morning," Ben answers, as if it was perfectly normal for him to be there.

"Um...what are you doing?"

He strains his neck to see me around the hood of my car. "Replacing your battery."

The concept is very strange to me. "Just like that?"

"Just like that." He releases the stabilizing rod and lets the hood slam down hard.

"Like magic. Suddenly I have a new battery," I say sarcastically.

He gathers up his tools and stops to look at me, trying to gauge my mood. "Well, it was either replace the battery, so we don't have to worry about you driving this thing, or dust off that old farm truck and see if it's in any better running condition."

I glance over at the rusty farm truck on the other side of the garage. I can't believe my pops would keep it all these years. My phone starts to ring, and I hold up one finger to pause him while I answer. "It's Etienne."

He drops the tools into the bed of the truck with a loud thud and scrunches up his face as if he's just swallowed something sour. "Who?"

I hold my hand over the speaker of the phone. "My boyfriend."

Ben closes the tailgate and listens curiously.

"Bonjour, Cheri."

"Hi, I've been hoping to hear from you."

"I'm sorry, I was working," Etienne claims.

Ben begins to grin. "Etienne sounds like some kind of a rash or something."

I give him an annoyed look and try to walk away, but he follows.

"The funeral was yesterday. I really needed you."

Ben leans against the side of the truck and continues to tease me, "I had to get me a prescription cream for this Etienne on my backside."

I wave him away. "Stop it," I warn in a whisper.

He chuckles. "All right, I'll leave you be." He gets into his truck and makes his way around the circular driveway past the house.

I get an uneasy feeling. "Who's with you?"

"Nobody," he denies.

I distinctly heard a woman's voice and it sure didn't sound like she was discussing business.

"Can you hold the line?" He places me on hold, without waiting for a reply. Bright red brake lights catch my attention, and I watch as Ben's truck skids to a hard stop on the dirt driveway. He gets out and stands, with his hands on his head, staring at the rubble at the front door. "What the hell happened?" he hollers, as he turns to face me.

"Aliens...tornado...zombie apocalypse." I roll my eyes. "What do you think happened?"

He grumbles and steps over the wreckage, picking up boards and inspecting them as he goes. Growing impatient with waiting on Etienne, I disconnect the call.

"It's completely rotten!" I hear Ben exclaim as I walk toward him. His brow furrows and he walks quickly toward me. My heart races nervously as he reaches down and takes hold of my wrist and lifts my arm. "Is that how you got these cuts and bruises?"

I tug my wrist, trying to break free of his grasp. "It's nothing. I'm fine."

He releases me and scowls. "There's a splinter of wood in one. We need to get it out before it festers and gets infected."

I look down at the red, puffy abrasion and cringe. "There's a first aid kit in the house, under the kitchen sink."

Ben follows me to the door and shakes his head in disapproval as I step up onto the bucket. "It'll do for now," I reason, as I open the door.

"Isn't your aunt coming to visit?"

I hadn't thought of that. "Yes, the day before I leave."

Ben looks around at the rotten wood piles and then back at the bucket.

"I'll figure something out," I assure him. "There's no rain in the forecast for the next few days. Maybe I'll just plan a picnic outside."

"You want her to go through the house contents and take the things that have family value," he reminds me, as he follows me into the house. It's annoying that he thinks of everything. And clearly, he has a knack for listening to other people's conversations.

I ignore him and put the rusty, metal, first aid container on the counter.

Ben looks at it and then at me. "It looks like it's from the first World War."

"Knowing my nana, it probably is."

He rummages through it, pulling out some tweezers and a small bottle of antiseptic.

"Are you sure you know what you're doing?"

"I'm a carpenter by trade." He holds my arm up, looking at it in better light. "I've removed more than a few wood splinters in my day."

"Good to know."

"I need a needle or a pin."

I raise my brow. "Do I want to know what for?"

"Trust me."

There's something in those baby blue eyes that puts me at ease. "Nana's sewing box is still beside her chair in the living room."

"Stay here," he instructs as he leaves the room.

I look down at an incoming text from Etienne.

Etienne: Sorry, something came up. I'll call you later.

When Ben returns to the room, I turn my phone upside down, not wanting him to see my messages. He gives me a curious look as he uses an alcohol wipe to sterilize a pin. "Okay, don't move." He uses it to gently pry away the skin, until he has uncovered enough of the splinter to get a hold of it with the tweezers. I look away. "The tricky part is making sure it all comes out in one piece."

I cringe, but my eyes flit back to watch his masculine hand care for my injury in a tender way. I don't think there's a girl in the world who wouldn't melt when her man cares for her in this manner.

"There. All done," he says, interrupting my thoughts.

I look down at my arm. "That's it?"

"That's it." He peels the backing off a bandage and sticks it over the small open wound, and gently caresses it to make sure it sticks. When he lifts his eyes to mine, something passes between us. There's a brief pause and I feel my face flush. "Thank you," I finally force myself to say, as I quickly try to put some distance between us.

He follows me into the living room. "It's a beautiful home."

"It used to be." I look around at the dusty furniture and the piles of stuff that has accumulated.

"It's a little clutter and dirt," he adds, noticing my frown. "It won't take much to return her to her former glory."

"I was thinking more that I was going to have to put her out of her misery." I can tell by the look on his face that I've just offended him.

"You wouldn't consider something that drastic, would you?"

I shrug. "I'm only here for a few more days."

"Then what?"

"Then I'm heading back to France."

"To Etchin," he says, holding my attention.

I ignore his intentional mispronunciation. "Yes, and my job."

"It must be a very important job."

Something in his tone irks me. "It is," I say defensively.

"What kind of work do you do?"

"Marketing." I saunter around the living room, picking up knick-knacks and dusting them off.

"Aren't there marketing jobs here?"

I laugh once. "Here? In Mono Mills?"

"Why does that seem like such a strange notion to you? We're only forty-five minutes from all the larger cities. Entrepreneurs are moving into town everyday with new ideas and dreams. Artists, bed and breakfast operators, investors, merchants, and restaurateurs are moving into the area and have found a way to improve our cultural footprint."

I suppose he's right, but I hadn't considered it. Living in France has been my dream ever since I travelled there on a school trip when I was fifteen. His unwavering glare makes me feel uncomfortable.

"So what is your plan for the house then?" he asks.

I pick up my pops' favourite picture of Nana and stare at it. "I don't know, really." I frown and put it back in its place. "Sell it, I guess." I can feel Ben watching me from the other side of the room. His silence heightens the feelings of guilt I get every time I think about it. "I need to pay off Pops' debt and settle the estate," I reason.

Ben looks at me as if I've just broken his heart.

"There's no other way?"

"None that I can think of."

He gives me a slight nod. "I've got chores to do. I better get going." His somber expression darkens my mood.

I watch from the kitchen window as he drives away and wonder how many times my nana stood here gazing out this window. My heart starts to flutter as an inexplicable warmth surrounds me, and I get a tight feeling around my body, like I've just been hugged.

It's likely because I'm exhausted, but I quicken my pace as I pass the door to my mother's room, certain I hear fluttering. It's amazing how a mind can play tricks on you when you're all alone, out in the country, in the dark...where nobody would hear you scream.

As I lie in bed, I'm bothered by the look on Ben's face when he left. I can't get him out of my mind. I've known the man for less than a week, and yet I'm losing sleep over disappointing him. There's something about him that draws me in and makes me feel...I don't really know what the feeling is, or maybe I don't want to acknowledge it. I haven't acknowledged my feelings for Etienne either. Why is it so hard for me to say *I love you*? I roll over, facing away from the door and ignoring the strange creaking sound I just heard out in the hallway. I need to get some sleep. I've got a million things to do in the next few days before I head home to France, and tomorrow, I have an appointment with an accountant to get the finances in order.

CHAPTER SIX

On Monday morning, I sit across the desk from a rather intense looking woman, as she flips through a stack of documents in front of her and keys figures into a spreadsheet on her computer at an impressive speed.

"So if I wanted to keep the house," I ask nervously, "What would be the amount of debt I need to pay off?"

"I would like to go over the numbers more thoroughly, and ensure that we've received all the claims of debt, but at this moment this is the figure."

She scribbles a number on a piece of paper and pushes it across the table toward me. I feel my jaw drop. "How is that possible?"

She thumbs through the bills in front of her. "It appears the largest part of the debt is additional mortgages on the property that he used for equipment repairs, land taxes, a trip to France, and school loans..."

I furrow my brow. "Wait, what? School loans for what? Pops said my tuition was covered by educational funds and scholarships set up by the family."

She slides a stack of paperwork across the table to me. I skim through the invoices and statements from the university, becoming tense and aggravated. "Oh, Pops." I shake my head in disbelief. "I had no idea he was mortgaging the farm to pay for my school."

"From the ledgers he kept, the land he leased didn't even cover the property taxes."

I close my eyes and sigh.

"If you'd like my advice, I suggest you sell it. As soon as possible. Liquidate any assets and pay off all the outstanding debt. Take what's left and go on a dream vacation. Put it all behind you."

"Put it all behind me. That was her advice," I say into phone as I drive home feeling agitated.

"You are using hands-free I hope, darling."

"Yes, of course." I fumble as I put the call on speaker and try to balance it on the dash as I drive.

"It sounds like good advice," Etienne says, sounding rather uncaring. "She's an accountant, she would have experience with these kinds of things."

"Put what behind me? My childhood? My memories? My grandparents?"

"No! Of course not! Sweetheart, don't be upset. France is home now, yes?"

I hesitate. "Yes."

"Then what choice do you have? Keep the farm and do what? Rent it out? Can you afford to pay off the debt?"

"No."

"Call an agent and have the house appraised. Then decide. Will I see you soon?"

"I'll be home day after tomorrow. I land in the late afternoon."

"Delightful, be a good girl and send me your flight details, will you? Shall I pick you up?"

"No, I left my car at the parking service."

"Will I see you for dinner?"

"If you're at the office, yes."

"You're not going to go home?"

"No, I need to get some stuff done at the office."

"Cora, you're going to be exhausted."

"I'm already emotionally exhausted. I really need to get back to work and get my mind off things." And by *things*, I mean more than the house and my grandfather's debt.

I pull into my driveway and sigh. Just once, it would be nice to arrive home and not have strange people here. There's a sizeable fire burning in the firepit, and a young teenage boy throws what looks like the rotten wood and debris from the fallen porch onto it. A man I recognize from the funeral unloads a few planks of timber from the back of a pickup truck.

"Hi," I say awkwardly as I walk toward him.

"Jeff," he offers. "That's my son, Caleb."

I smile. "What's going on?"

"Caleb's gonna hang out for a few hours and help clean up the mess from the old porch. I'm just dropping some stuff off for Jake and Ben."

"Where are they?"

"In the barn. Making stringers for the steps."

A warm feeling washes over me. I don't get these kinds of feelings in France. Between work and avoiding conversations with people on the train, I don't really socialize much. Even the nights that Etienne and I share a few glasses of wine and a fancy dinner, one or both of us is still answering emails or working out marketing plans for upcoming campaigns. I stand at the barn door watching the two brothers measure and mark the wood, ensuring that every cut is perfect.

Jake looks up and sees me first.

"Hi," he says, lifting his safety glasses.

"Hi." I cross my arms. "What are you doing?"

"Ben was worried about your aunt getting into the house. We thought we should put up a quick set of steps, so she'd be safe."

I nod. "So did it ever occur to you to ask me if I wanted steps built?"

"Nope," Ben adds while marking the cross angle on the board he's working on.

"Maybe, a phone call first?" I add.

"I don't have your number," he says with his head down.

"Well, why would you need my number when you're always here?" I say sarcastically.

Ben stops and looks up, finally acknowledging me. "You don't want us to build steps so your aunt can get into the house safely? Is that what I'm hearing?"

"Yes." Now, I feel like an asshole. "No. That's not what I mean. I just mean that..." I give up. "Can I pay you for the material and work?"

Jake shakes his head no. "We called in some favours owed."

"Can I help?"

"You can get me a beer," Ben requests.

I give him an unimpressed look.

"Geez," he says to Jake. "It's a good thing I didn't ask for a sandwich."

It helps that I'm starting to dislike this guy. Maybe those other *unidentified* feelings will go away. "I don't have any beer."

"In the cooler, in the back of my truck." He turns on the power to the saw and continues his work. Jake puts in his order by holding one finger in the air. I nod my acknowledgement as I walk to the truck, open the cooler, and take out three beers. I haven't had a beer in a long time. Dinner in France is usually enjoyed with wine. The grinding hum of the saw comes to a stop, and I notice my phone is ringing.

"Hi, Cora. This is Lynn. Beatrice's PSW. She's been feeling a little under the weather so I'm afraid we're not going to make it out tomorrow."

"Oh no. I hope it's not too serious."

"The doctor was just in and he thinks it's pneumonia, he's ordered some tests and wants to keep a close watch on her."

"Of course. I totally understand. Unfortunately, I fly home to France tomorrow night at midnight, so I won't get to see her."

"Will you be back?"

I hear cursing as I walk back to the barn. "I'm not sure when, but I'll have to come back and pack up all the stuff in the house."

"Have a safe flight. Keep in touch."

"Thank you, I will. And please keep me posted about Aunt Bea."

I hang up and hand Ben his beer. "What's wrong?"

"We've got no power."

"Did you blow a breaker?"

"Oh, well...there's a thought," Ben says, mocking me. "Hey, Jake! Did you think to check the breaker?"

Jake's brows snap together as he takes the last beer out of my hand. "Stop being such an ass. You know I did."

"So what's the problem then?" I wonder.

"Have you paid the bills?" Ben says in jest.

I raise my eyebrows. "Uhhh. I don't know. I haven't paid anything since I got here. They wouldn't just shut things off, would they?"

"I don't think so," Jake assures me. "They would have sent notices in the mail first."

I close my eyes and frown.

"Have you been checking the mailbox at the end of the road?" Ben asks. "You know, out here they still delivery paper envelopes into those funny shaped boxes to the old folks who don't bank online."

I feel my body tense and my face turn red. "I didn't think about it!" I say defensively.

Ben shakes his head and walks to the open barn door. "Caleb!" he hollers. "Run down and fetch the mail from the box."

I avoid eye contact with him at all cost, while we drink our beers and wait in silence for the boy to return. I stand erect, feeling alarmed as he jogs up to the barn, with his arms full.

"I'll go back and make sure I didn't drop anything," he pants, as he plops the stack of letters and flyers on the hood of the tractor. Ben glances over at me, but I ignore him as he sorts through the papers and holds up an envelope. *Final Notice* it says in large red letters on the outside.

"Fuck," I curse aloud.

"There's your answer."

"Well, how was I supposed to know he was in arrears on everything?" I say, on the verge of breaking down. "It's not like he kept me in the loop on anything. He didn't even tell me about the cancer."

"See what you've done?" Jake scolds Ben. "You've upset her. Why do you have to be such a dick? What would our mother think if she knew you were making girls cry? She's probably rolling over in her grave right now."

Ben sighs and wraps his arms around me in a firm hug. "I'm sorry, Cora."

At the moment, I'm not questioning the comfort I feel when I'm firmly planted against his chest with his strong arms surrounding me. "What do I do now?"

"We'll go home and get some gas for the generator and hope it starts. It probably hasn't been used for many years."

"It's after hours, so you can't deal with the hydro company until tomorrow anyway," Jake adds.

I wipe the dampness from my cheeks. "While you do that, I think I'm going to drive out to the old cemetery and see Nana. I want to do that before I go back to France tomorrow."

"We'll take Caleb home and be here when you get back," Jake assures me.

"Be careful out there," Ben warns. "It's gonna be dark soon and that cemetery, including the roads leading to it, aren't well maintained."

I feel a little glimmer of hope for him. "Are you worried about me, Ben?"

He tries to hide an amused grin. "Nah, I just don't have time for another rescue mission."

It's a short drive on winding country roads through the beautiful hills of Mono. I connect my Bluetooth and make a call.

"Hello, Fiona?"

"Yes."

"My name is Cora Scott. Gordon Henderson gave me your number. He thought you might be able to help me out with a property I've inherited."

"How is Gordon?" she asks cheerfully.

"He seems fine."

"That's great! How can I help?"

"I'd like to get the place appraised."

"Are you thinking of selling?"

"Yes. No." I pause. "I live in France now, so I believe I have no other option but sell. It's just that the place has a lot of sentimental value to me. It's where I grew up."

"I understand. When do you go back to France?"

"I'm leaving tomorrow."

"That poses a problem."

"Well, I'm thinking we might be able to handle all the details remotely. If you could just go out to the house and have a look at the property when you have time in the next week and give me an idea of what I'm looking at?"

"Is it vacant?"

"Nobody is living there currently. It is a little bit *rustic*. There haven't been many upgrades to the house. I've packed up a few boxes of things, but as of right now, all my grandparents' belongings are still there."

"Sometimes places sell better when they're not completely empty. If we get it sold, there are companies who can pack it all up and send it to you in France."

"Really?"

"You can hire someone to do anything if you have the money. You might even be able to hold an auction at the house and liquidate the stuff you know you don't want."

"Will you be able to go out to the property and have a look around?"

"Yes, I can do that toward the end of the week."

"Thank you, I'll email you the location of the spare key and the phone number in France where I can be reached."

I end the call at the perfect time, as I pull up to the historic church cemetery. The original stone and mortar church still stands staunchly on high ground. Only problem with having a cemetery in this county is all the graves are practically downhill. The gates are locked, so I park at the bottom of the road and find an opening in the fence to squeeze through. I need to bump up my cardio when I get back to France, this incline is killing me. I'm glad Nana is buried midway up the hill. The view from here is breathtaking, nonetheless.

It takes me a few minutes to catch my breath as I stand at the base of the three plots purchased by my grandfather. My grandmother was laid to rest here when she passed, and the empty one at the end is meant for Aunt Beatrice when it's time. I study the grave in between them that was meant to be my pops. The tombstone bears an unfamiliar name, and it bothers me that a stranger resides here.

"Good news, Nana. Pops will be moving in as soon as the ground has thawed enough. Be sure you make him knock the mud off his boots." Normally I'd like to sit awhile and chat with Nana, but there's someone else I want to visit today.

I climb higher and wander up and down a few rows. I don't know exactly where she is, since I've never actually visited my mother's grave. It was something that caused my grandparents a lot of pain and so they didn't come here often, and when they did, they didn't bring me. As a child I never thought much about it until Nana passed, then I became curious. The day of her funeral, I dug down deep and found the courage to ask Pops where my mother was buried. I could tell he didn't want to tell me, when he reluctantly waved in this direction. Feeling like I would be betraying him somehow, I didn't look for her that day.

A monarch butterfly whisks past me and I'm compelled to follow it, as if it's guiding me. It lands on a tombstone and I stop to read the inscription. Here I stand, face-to-face with her after all these years. I've heard of stories of people who thought loved ones were dead, only to discover that they simply wished to disappear, or their existence was hidden by others for some distorted reason or another. I never doubted my momma was dead, but staring at her name chiseled in marble makes it *real*.

There's a bouquet of fresh flowers on the ground and I stare at them a long while, watching the petals dance in the wind. At first, I thought they may have blown here, but as I look around at the surrounding, unkempt graves I realize someone has been tending to my mother; and quite recently it seems. These flowers were meant for her. I brush my fingertips along her name and read the dates. It's hard to believe that she was only nineteen when she died.

I regret not asking my grandparents about her death. No matter how upset and angry they got, I should have just kept asking until they told me the truth. I close my eyes. I was only two and a half years old when she died, but I remember her smile, her voice, her love. Or maybe I just want to have pleasant memories, so I've fabricated some for myself from the photos in the album. I guess I'll never know for sure. I decide I like these happy memories, so I choose to believe them.

I'm disappointed I won't see Aunt Bea before I go back to France; I have so many questions. As I walk back to the car it begins to get dark and a strange feeling washes over me as I make my way down the hillside. I hesitate a moment before getting in my car, feeling as if I'm being watched. My pulse starts to race. It's time to get out of here.

I'm relieved to see Jake and Ben are still at the house, but I'd never tell them that.

I finish booking my transport to the airport and I smile getting out of the vehicle, as I notice their father is also with them. "You're still here! And you've brought reinforcements."

"Yup," Ben says, looking up and then doing a double take as if he's never seen a girl smile.

"Nice to see you again, Phil."

"I thought I'd come over and help."

"Good thing you did, Dad. Or we would have never gotten that generator going."

"Bah, you would have figured it out," he says bashfully.

"You've been at it for hours; you must be starving. Do you want to stay for supper?"

"Thanks anyway," Phil says, as he brushes the sawdust off his clothes. "We've got chores to do at home."

I pout. "Now I really feel bad."

"Don't," Ben adds. "At least your aunt will be safe when she comes to visit."

"Ohhhhhhh yeah, *that*." I scrunch up my face and Ben gives me a look.

"What?"

"She called earlier."

"And?"

I avoid eye contact with him when I say it. "She's not coming. She's sick."

"I'm sorry to hear that," Jake says sympathetically. "I hope it's nothing serious."

"Everything at our age is serious," Phil adds.

Ben nods. "You're probably right."

"They think it's pneumonia. I'm sorry, I meant to tell you, but I got distracted."

"Let's go," Ben grumbles to his father, obviously annoyed with me. "It's getting late."

"I'd come and help you with your chores, for a change, but I need to finish packing to go home."

"You're going back tomorrow?" Phil asks. "But you just got home. Can't you stay longer?"

"No, I'm sorry, I can't. I have to go back to work. I could only get a week off."

Jake watches Ben's reaction.

"What time is your flight?" Phil asks.

"Something stupid like 12:08 a.m. I have to meet the airport shuttle at a pickup point in town at eight."

"On the twenty-third?"

"No, the twenty-second."

Jake raises his eyebrows. "Are you sure?"

"Yes, I'm sure." I get my phone out of my pocket to double-check anyway.

"Well, if you've arranged airport transportation to pick you up at eight tomorrow evening, you're gonna be late for your flight," Ben adds.

"What are you talking about? I only need to be there three hours before an international flight."

Ben purses his lips and goes back to what he was doing. I look at Jake, confused.

Phil scratches his head. "Well, I'm not sure how to tell you this, but today is the twenty-first."

"Yes, I know that."

"12:08 a.m. on the twenty-second of May means your flight's leaving in..." Jake looks at his watch, "three and a half hours." He raises his shoulders in a half shrug. Panic washes over me as I double-check the date, time, and itinerary. He's right.

"Oh, for fuck's sakes!" I throw my head back in distress. "How could I have got it that mixed up?"

I dial the airbus customer service line and hold the phone to my ear, as I run into the house. I'm on the third step when I stop and turn with a look of terror.

"I forgot there's no power. How am I supposed to find anything?"

"The generator is still hooked to the house, so you've got enough power to put some lights on." Jake advises.

"You can do that?"

"You can do that when the main hydro box has the proper connection for the generator," Phil says.

"Thank you," I say relieved.

Ben ignores me and puts his tools in the back of his truck, looking defeated. I hesitate, wishing it didn't bother me to see him that way.

I rush around the house throwing my clothes and personal items into the old trunk while still waiting on hold. Finally, somebody answers.

"Hi, I have a bit of an urgent situation. I just booked transport for tomorrow night. The last name is Scott. I had the wrong date. I need to leave to the airport tonight. Like...right now!"

"I'm sorry, Miss Scott. We don't have a service that could come and pick you up, and tonight's shuttle has already left the pickup point. You might want to try a private service or a cab."

"There are no cabs out this way that will go to the airport!" I fumble with the phone while I try to continue packing. "There must be something you can do?"

"I'm sorry, I've cancelled your transport for tomorrow and refunded the money to your credit card. If you decide to reschedule your flight to a later date, please call us back to rebook."

"Reschedule my flight?" I panic and start to hyperventilate when I realize she's disconnected the call.

"Cora, take a breath."

I look over my shoulder at Ben standing in the doorway and try to calm my anxiety.

"Breathe," he instructs. "Jake and I will drive you to the airport."

I search for the words to turn down his offer, but he's aware of my apprehension.

"It's okay," he assures me. "Dad has taken Jake's truck back to the house, and I'll pay Caleb to come out and help us catch up on chores tomorrow."

I continue to stare at him, looking stunned. There are a lot of reasons I should just cancel this flight and stay, and right now Ben is one of them. But I can't, I have to return home to France. Work is expecting me and so is Etienne.

"Well, if you're not gonna say anything, could you at least point at the things you're taking so I can put them in the truck?"

I finally feel like I can breathe. "Sorry. Just this one." I slam the lid down on the old trunk and try to latch it. It frustrates me that it won't close. Ben steps up to help me, and I feel a shiver across my skin as he brushes against me. I try to ignore it, but I feel my face start to flush with colour. Ben pauses with an ardent expression, and I know he felt it too. He lifts the lid of the trunk and tucks all the straggling pieces of clothing inside. This time when he shuts it, it latches tight.

"Why are you using this old thing anyway?" he grunts, as he drags it off the bed. "It's got to be heavier than the stuff you're taking in it."

"I know. It belonged to my mother, and I just can't bring myself to part with it. It gave me comfort to have part of her with me when I moved to France. I was going to buy a new one for my next trip, but it came up rather unexpectedly." I expect Ben to have some harsh words, but he surprises me.

"I can understand that you wanted to keep a connection with your home while you were so far away."

I smile until he continues his thought and ruins the moment.

"You couldn't have taken something lighter, like a hanky or a photo?"

As I lock the door, Jake turns off the generator and then helps Ben lift the trunk into the back of the truck. I feel a burdensome weight on me as we leave for the airport, and I take one last look at the house. A strange glow reflects in the kitchen window and a thought hits me. "Wait" I scream.

Ben hits the brakes and the two brothers look at me shocked. "I forgot my passport." I jump out of the truck and run back to the house. I fumble to get the door unlocked but finally it opens. I hit the switch, forgetting that there's no longer any power to the house and have to use my phone to guide me to the table where I left it. I pick it up and pause a moment, then shine the light around the room. When I spot the only picture of my mother that Nana would let me have, I grab it, remove it from the frame, and take it with me.

As we drive out of town, I carefully place the picture in my wallet.

"So what about the rest of the stuff you've left behind?" Ben asks, as we turn off the dirt road onto the main highway into the city. "Are you coming back?"

"The real estate lady suggested that I could hire someone to pack it all up or have an auction to get rid of it."

"You'd do that? Sell everything off?"

I pause a moment. "It sounded like a good idea at the time. Honestly, there's so much about my family that I don't know. I'd like to spend some time with Aunt Beatrice and find out what the history is behind some of those things my nana held on to. Maybe their worth something, or maybe they were just precious to her. I lay awake some nights wondering."

"So why are you leaving?"

"I could only get a week of vacation from work." I watch the blurred lights of the cars on the highway as Ben speeds past them. "I didn't know I was going to have so many *complications* when I got here."

Ben looks at me in the rearview mirror. "So you're going to sell the house and stay in France with Chretien."

"Etienne," I correct.

"Whatever."

Now I'm getting angry. "You know, you've got an awful lot of opinions about my life choices and the decisions I should make. I've only known you a week."

"Mono Mills is home. It's where you belong," he says with little emotion in his tone.

"And what about my career? Etienne? Oh wait…" I say with an offended tone. "Look who I'm talking to."

"Doesn't seem to me like you love the guy. Not really. He seems like a scumbag. What kind of man doesn't travel with his woman when she's lost a family member?" he asks, looking at Jake for affirmation.

"What would you know about love?" I scoff. "Have you ever loved *anything*?"

Jake looks over his shoulder at me and his eyes open wide as he shakes his head slightly in warning. Angst washes over his expression as he glances at Ben, waiting for his reaction. Instead there's an uncomfortable silence that remains until we take the exit into the airport and arrive at Terminal 3 departures.

Jake jumps out and unloads my trunk from the back of the truck. I look in the window, to say goodbye to Ben, but he holds onto the steering wheel with white knuckles and stares straight ahead looking wounded.

I frown. "I've hit a nerve."

"A big one," Jake admits.

"I should apologize."

"No. Let it go. He'll be fine." He pulls me into his arms and gives me a firm hug. "Have a safe trip. If you make it back to town, be sure to let us know."

"I will. I just don't know right now what I'm going to do. There's so much to figure out."

"I know." He releases me and looks around me, into the truck window. "He's not a bad guy, you know. He's had a rough go himself. Believe me...he likes you. Otherwise he wouldn't have such strong opinions."

I turn to find Ben staring at me. I have no idea what battle he's fought, but I have no right to judge him either. Me and my big mouth.

"You better get going. You're short on time as it is," Jake reminds me as he tucks a folded piece of paper into my hand. "If you tell him I gave it to you, I'll deny it."

I furrow my brow. "Okay."

Determined not to leave with bad feelings between us, I tap on the window until Ben acknowledges me and I mouth the words, '*Thank you.*' I feel a small amount of relief from my guilt when he nods his acknowledgement before hitting the gas and squealing the tires as he pulls away. I unfold the paper, and laugh, looking up to watch the tail lights of the truck fade out of sight. Scribbled on the note is Ben's name and phone number with a message that reads *For a good time, call.*

CHAPTER SEVEN

It's nothing short of a miracle that I get my luggage checked in and get through security and customs. I arrive at my gate a few moments before boarding. I've got time to call Etienne and let him know I'm on my way home a day early. I try the number twice, but the signal in the airport is so weak it won't connect. The red battery light begins to flash, warning that it needs to be recharged. I frantically look for my charging cable, but I can't find it. I throw my head back in frustration when I realize it's still plugged into the wall socket in the kitchen.

I spot a small corner store just up the entrance way. I'll buy a new one. I rush as quickly as I can through the crowds and grab the cord I need. I fidget impatiently in the line of several people waiting to check out. Over the loudspeaker I hear a muffled announcement, "Attention, passengers. Would Cora Scott please report to Gate B? This is last call for boarding Flight 779 to France."

Crap. I drop the cord on top of the nearest candy display and run as quickly as I can. I can see the flight attendants gathering up their paperwork and closing the gate. "Wait!" I yell. "Wait! I'm here."

A rather stunning looking redhead with meticulously coiffed hair looks up at me and waves me over. She takes my passport and boarding pass out of my hand and scans it. "Quickly! They're waiting for you." I run down the narrow connecting tunnel toward the plane and see a young girl watching for me. She waves me in. I gasp for air as she closes the heavy door behind me.

"That was a close one," I pant.

She smiles. "You have no idea how often that happens. Welcome aboard. I'll show you to your seat."

I squeeze my way down the narrow aisle on what looks to be a sold-out flight. I take my seat beside a rather large, sweaty man. He tries to move over as far as he can to give me more space. I give him a polite smile, but I know this is going to be a very long seven-hour flight. I stuff my bag under the seat and stow my phone in the pocket in front of me. As the plane takes off, I find myself thinking about Ben and I wonder why he was so hurt by what I said. From Jake's reaction, someone must have broken his heart.

I think hard about the comments he made about Etienne. I'd dismiss it as some twisted male jealousy thing, if I hadn't had the same thoughts myself. We keep our relationship very private, since we both work with the same firm. Normally, I wouldn't entertain the idea of an office romance, and he came off as sort of a player, but he was persistent. If he didn't love me, he wouldn't be pushing for me to move in with him. The only thing left for me in Mono Mills is memories and mysteries. Once the house is sold, maybe I can finally move on to the next phase of my relationship with Etienne. Who knows, maybe one day, I'll even be able to say, 'I love you.'

Once we're in the air, I take another look through my bag for a phone charger but come up empty. I open my wallet and slide out the picture of my mother and stare at it for a very long time. We have the same smile and wavy brown hair. I'm practically her mini-me except for our eyes. Hers a brilliant blue that sparkled like sapphires; mine a rich dark brown with flecks of gold. As I drift into sleep, I begin to recall one of the earliest memories I have of her.

My momma looks beautiful in her pastel green dress and the oversized straw Easter hat. She wipes the maple syrup off my face before running the comb through my curls. I stare at her in the mirror, trying to memorize every single detail of her warm, loving smile. It's almost as if I knew, that one day, her smile would be gone forever.

After church, Nana prepares a huge ham dinner while Momma and I change into our jeans and boots. When we get out to the living room, she hands me a small, brightly decorated wicker basket. "Now, we're going to collect eggs."

I'm confused because this is not the basket we use to collect the eggs, but I head out to the chicken coop with it anyway.

"Do you know what today is?" she asks me.

I nod my head. "Easter."

"Do you know who comes Easter morning?"

"Jesus," I announce proudly.

My mom smiles and plays with my curls. "I'm talking about the Easter bunny. Do you know what the Easter bunny does?"

I shake my head no, and wait, wide-eyed for the story.

"The Easter bunny comes, and he hides brightly decorated eggs for us to find."

"Why?" I ask innocently.

"Bunnies and eggs are symbols for new life. The Easter bunny paints them up all bright and beautiful to help us celebrate spring and all that's coming back to life." She points at the cluster of spring flowers blooming in the middle of the grass. "Shall we look to see if he hid any eggs?"

My eyes sparkle with excitement. "Okay!" I practically run into the chicken coop, and I can hear my momma laughing as I slide my hand under one of the big red hens, pull out a bright pink egg, and open my eyes wide in amazement. We find half a dozen coloured eggs when the coop door opens, and a stream of bright light shines through.

"What ya still doing in here?" Pops asks. "A little bunny told me that there's chocolate eggs hidden in the barn."

I gasp and my momma smiles.

"Eggs made out of chocolate?" I scream.

"Dad, you shouldn't have done that, we don't have the money for that kind of stuff," she whispers.

"Nonsense. Let her be a little girl."

In my childhood innocence, I have no idea what they're talking about. I turn to see her give him a tight hug as she passes by him and follows me into the barn. The Easter bunny did the perfect job hiding shiny foil covered eggs in the barn. There's only a few; but they're strategically placed at just the right height for a two-year-old. I grab a handful off the bumper of that rusty old farm truck and put them in my basket, one by one, feeling a great sense of pride that I've discovered the most wonderful treasure.

My eyes open as the plane begins to make its final descent into Paris. I reach for my phone, but it's now completely dead. I discreetly peek through the seats in front of me at the time on someone's phone. I do the math in my head. Unloading, luggage, time change, car retrieval and traffic. I should be home around dinner time. I won't worry about calling Etienne at this point. I'll just show up and surprise him and tell him I've decided, once the house sells, I'll get out of the lease on my apartment and move in.

I begin to get excited as I drive to his place just outside of Paris. And even more excited when I see his car parked in its usual spot. I can't wait to see him. I leave everything in my car in a hurry to surprise him. I take the stairs, two at a time, to the second floor and stand at the door. Adrenaline and excitement make my hand tremble as I knock. I wait...and wait. I put my ear to the door, before digging out my key and opening it. The radio is playing so he's probably in the shower.

His briefcase is in its usual spot at the front door and the bathroom door is open, but the shower isn't on. I walk across the room and turn off the stereo. I hear it immediately. Sounds that make my blood run like sour milk through my veins. I walk to the closed bedroom door and stop to listen. I hold the doorknob, hesitating, while I listen to the passionate moaning of a woman on the other side. When I hear the well-known growl of Etienne's voice, I turn the knob and open the door. It takes him a few moments to notice that I'm standing there. He is busy, after all, pleasuring his secretary. My stomach turns upside down, and I feel like I'm about to throw up when he finally looks over to see me standing there. "Cora!"

Speechless, I slam the bedroom door and hurry to leave. By the time I get to the top of the stairwell, he opens the door and calls my name as he pulls on a pair of pants and chases me. He catches up to me as I start my car and put it in gear. He attempts to get in front of me to stop me from leaving, but I hit the gas, making him jump out of the way. I glance in my rearview mirror and see him watching me, with his hands on his head in the middle of the street.

I roll down the window to get some air as I drive to the apartment I rent on the other side of town. I'm in such a fog that I'm not even sure how I get there. One of the wheels jams as I pull the heavy trunk off the elevator, and I drag it the rest of the way up the hall making one hell of a noise. I apologize to the neighbours who poke their heads out their doors to see what all the commotion is. The moment I get it far enough inside my apartment to close the door, I plop myself down on top of it. Once the tears start to flow, I can't stop; I break down into a hard sob.

I reach into my pocket, looking for a tissue and pull out the folded paper with Ben's number on it. I toss it on the coffee table as I sit on the couch. I don't know how long I sit there before I plug in my phone. When it finally charges enough to come back to life, I look down at thirty missed calls from Etienne. I delete the notifications and block his calls. Then I delete and block him from all social media. I'm sure nobody knew about us. Etienne insisted that we kept it private, since office romances were not encouraged. Now I know it had nothing to do with him valuing his career; he was still playing the field. I should have seen this coming. Things are going to be awkward at the office tomorrow. Serves me right for thinking the office Casanova was capable of a monogamous relationship. I guess the joke's on me.

I lie in bed and watch movies on television until almost 11:00 p.m. The time difference has me really messed up, so despite being emotionally exhausted I'm not quite ready to sleep. Lying in the dark, I feel like that little girl who's all alone in the world again. And I suppose this time I actually am.

I've just closed my eyes when the alarm screams to life. In a fog, I get ready for work and get on the train. I stare out the window at the blurred mass of people making their way into the city for their daily grind. My pops used to tell me that every person you meet is fighting a battle you know nothing about, so it's just best to be kind. As I scan the crowded train car, looking at the people who are busy reading papers or on their phones, I wonder what battles they're fighting.

A man stands, and lets an older woman have his seat. When he reaches up to hold onto the bar to steady himself, I can see he has a sleeve of tattoos. It makes me think of Ben, and I wonder if he misses me. The train screeches to a halt at my stop. Excusing myself, I squeeze through the hoard of people and finally find myself out on the platform. I find it hard to breathe as I'm pushed and edged by the other passengers, trying to make their way up the stairs and into the city.

I can taste the exhaust from the traffic as cars idle in the standstill traffic jam. If I ever found this city charming and exciting, I don't today. The constant drone of the city construction and the chatter of the millions of people around me heightens my anxiety.

I'm on high alert when I enter my building and make my way to my office. If Etienne is here today, I pray he has the decency to leave me alone and not make a scene. I no sooner have the thought when he unexpectedly flanks me from the side and makes me jump.

"I called you many times."

"I blocked your number," I advise quietly, as I continue to walk.

"Can we talk?"

I laugh once as I turn to face him. "No."

"Please, Cherie. Let me explain."

I raise my brow. "Explain?" I continue walking to my office and he follows. "I don't think an explanation is needed."

"I'm sorry you saw that."

I smile and nod courteously to coworkers as they pass, pretending that nothing's wrong.

"You came home a day early," he continues.

I stop at my office door and turn, stopping him from following me in there alone. "Ah, so you're not sorry for cheating; you're sorry you got caught?" I feel the anger start to rip through my body, making my muscles tense.

Etienne glances up the hallway. "Perhaps this is a bad time to talk."

"There is no good time to talk."

"I love you."

That statement makes me feel sick, like I've just taken a punch to the stomach.

"No, Etienne. You don't. There's no possible way that you ever loved me."

A coworker comes up the hall with an armful of marketing mockup posters. "Five minutes in the boardroom," he advises as he passes.

"Give me another chance," Etienne pleads.

I shake my head, trying to comprehend what he's asking for. "Are you crazy? I came home to find you FUCKING one of your employees."

He shushes me and I feel the rage inside me start to build. "There is no possibility of me giving you another chance. Don't ever talk to me again."

He holds up his hand to silence me. "Okay, don't make a scene in our place of business."

Is he kidding me? I growl as I take a step back into my office and close the door. I press my palms against my temples, trying to quiet the pounding in my head. I'm hoping this anxious edgy feeling will enhance my creative spark today, or I might as well pack up my career and move on.

CHAPTER EIGHT

I throw myself into every open project, but the week still drags on. While some of my ideas are well liked by the clients, others are a huge fail. The constant roller-coaster ride begins to take its toll on me. I miss the fresh air and lush green rolling hills of home. I escape from the office and walk down to the small park a few blocks away. I brush the dirt off the only park bench and sit down. I'm part way through a ham sandwich and reading an email from Lynn about Aunt Bea's improving condition, when my phone rings. I answer quickly, since I've been waiting for her call.

"Hello, Cora. It's Fiona."

"Hi, I take it you've had a chance to get out to the house?"

"I did."

"And?"

"It needs a lot of work."

"Yes, it does. I believe I mentioned that to you."

"You did. You did."

"Do you think we can sell quickly?"

"Ya just never know," she says, sounding unconvinced. "If you could get some things looked after it would be better."

"Like?"

"Like updating the kitchen and the bathroom. Replace the flooring. Replace the roof. Paint the outside of the house. Put in new windows."

"Wait a minute," I interrupt, starting to feel overwhelmed. "As I mentioned, I'm in France."

"We can arrange for the work to be done. I have contractors I work with on a regular basis."

"Yes, but there's no money to do all those things. That farm *is* the estate."

"If you put the money into it now, you'll make it back when you sell the house. Maybe we can negotiate a down payment with some of the trades to get the work started, and pay the balance of the bill once the house sells."

"Maybe."

"I'll talk to my guy tomorrow. Now...what are you doing about clearing out all the clutter and giving it a good clean?"

"Do you have a *guy* for that?" I ask, starting to feel discouraged.

"I'll ask around."

"Could we not just sell it *as is*?"

"Honey, I can sell just about anything. But if you want a fair price for this property, you've got to work with me here."

I sigh. "Let me figure it out. I'll call you back. Could you please email me what you think the *as is* list value would be?"

"Sure. In the meantime, I'll start asking *around* to see who can take on a project this size right now."

I disconnect the call and take a bite of my ham sandwich. I've suddenly lost my appetite, so I toss it onto the grass and watch as the birds swarm to grab a few crumbs. Right now, I feel a lot like that crust of bread; everybody wants a piece of me but there's not enough to go around. It gives me a brilliant idea for one of our telecommunications campaigns, so I rush back to the office.

With a renewed excitement, I quickly work on the graphics and put together a mockup of the social media strategy and send it to my boss.

The next morning, I pump myself full of coffee, trying to jolt myself awake. It was a restless night with little sleep, so I keep my office door closed to discourage those who might stop by to chat. Something catches my attention outside of the closed glass door. Etienne stands in the hallway talking to the head of human resources. He doesn't look very happy right now. Security approaches him, and he turns to look right at me through the window. Not knowing what's going on, I look away until they've moved on.

I manage to remain undisturbed until mid-morning when there's a knock on the door and my boss, Marion Charles, walks in. I've always admired her. She made the climb up the corporate ladder at a time when women were still expected to stay home barefoot and pregnant. She's been with the company almost forty years; thirty of those as the director of marketing.

"How are you doing, dear?" she asks sincerely.

"I'm good. I'm all caught up, and I'm working on a few ideas..."

"I mean how are *you* doing?" she interrupts. "I understand you were raised by your grandparents. It must have been hard to go home and say goodbye."

I experience a moment of sorrow, with her concern. "It was. And things are such a mess there right now. I have so many loose ends to tie up."

She gives me a kind smile. "I'm sure you'll get it sorted out."

I nod. "I sent you my ideas for the Gateway Communications account."

"I saw them. And I loved it."

I feel relieved. "I'm glad."

"I have something I'd like to talk to you about."

I can't identify her tone so I'm unsure if it's something good or bad. "Of course," I say reluctantly.

"Don't worry," she says, noting my sudden uncomfortable disposition. "We suddenly have an opening for a marketing lead on the natural resources account."

I lower my brow, feeling confused. "That's Etienne's account."

"Yes, well it's come to my attention that Mr. Duval doesn't quite live up to the moral standards we take pride in here at Webster and Burnett. He and I have mutually agreed that it's time for him to move on."

I'm stunned. "You want me to take over?"

"Yes, I think you're ready for an account this size." She pushes her glasses to the top of her head. "Are you the right woman for the job, Miss Scott?"

I feel a rush of nervous excitement and I can't stop smiling. "Yes! I AM!" Without thinking, I throw myself at her and wrap her in a warm hug. She stiffens and pats me on the back. I suddenly realize what I'm doing. "Oh, I'm sorry," I say, feeling embarrassed as I pull away. "I don't know what got into me." I guess being back home in Canada, even for just a week, rubbed off on me. The people here aren't big on public displays of affection.

"Finish up any loose ends on the farm account and pass on any other files you're currently working on to one of the apprentices," she says as she turns to leave. "You won't have time for menial accounts now."

"Thank you, I won't let you down." I sit down and email all my files with lightning speed; afraid she may change her mind.

Angst pumps through my veins like a drug when I look up and see the last person I want to talk to right now. The timid girl cracks open the door and pokes her head in.

"Hi, Cora. Can I come in?"

This is turning out to be some day. The last time I saw her, she was underneath my boyfriend. I nod and sit back in my chair.

"I'm really sorry," she begins nervously. "I had no idea that you and he were in a relationship. I would never have gotten involved with him if I knew."

I hesitate a moment, looking at the blue-eyed, blonde-haired girl. There's something in her eyes that makes me believe her. "Let me guess. He left little notes on your desk for weeks, making you feel special, and when you finally agreed to go out with him, he told you how the company frowns on office romances so you should keep it a secret."

Her face flushes a bright shade of pink and tears well up in her eyes. "Yes."

I cuss and shake my head. "What an asshole." I get to my feet and pass her a tissue. "I hope you kicked that lying sack of shit to the curb."

"I did," she sniffles, as she dabs the moisture from her eyes.

"Good. You deserve better."

"Are you and I okay?"

I give her a sympathetic smile. "We are. I believe you didn't know."

Her shoulders relax and she lets out a sigh of relief. "Thank goodness. Etienne was fired, and I was just told you're my boss now. I was worried it would be kind of awkward."

"I imagine it could have been." I walk to the door, prompting her to follow me. "It's all good. Don't give it another thought." As she turns and leaves, I close the door and smile. *Boss*...I like the sound of that. It's what I've been working toward for a very long time.

I look at the time and round up everything on my desk and stuff it into my laptop bag. I leave work feeling a refreshed and renewed love for the city.

There's a cardboard box of my belongings in the hallway outside the door. My name is written on the outside flap in Etienne's handwriting. I unlock the door and push it inside with my foot. I'm not going to let my girl-brain ruin my exciting news. I pick up the box and shove it onto the crowded shelf in the front hall closet for now. I don't want to see it or deal with it today. Instead, I'm going to pop the cork on a very expensive bottle of French wine and pour a very large glass.

When I realize there's nobody to share my great news with, I feel deflated. I guess in the last twelve years I should have attempted to make some friends.

I'm at the bottom of the potent libation and in the mood to celebrate when I make a questionable choice.

"Hello"

"Hi, Ben."

"Cora?"

"Yes."

There's a small pause. "Is everything okay?"

"Yes, I'm fine."

"So why are you calling?" he asks suspiciously.

"I've got some great news! I've been put in charge of the largest account project the company has ever had."

"Congratulations."

I'm not sure if it's the wine, or the gruff sound of his voice that makes my stomach flutter. "Thank you."

"Your grandfather would have been proud of you," he adds.

I take a long, deep breath and refill my glass of wine. "Yes, he would have. Listen, Ben...I wanted to apologize about the night you drove me to the airport."

"It's okay."

"No, it's not. I crossed a line. You just make me so...crazy, sometimes."

"I'm pretty sure you were crazy before you met me," he jests.

I've been wondering about something since the night he drove me to the airport. "Have you ever been in love?" I ask, finding bravery in a few more sips of wine.

"I'm sure you'll find it hard to believe, but yes, I have."

"What happened?"

"It didn't work out. I ran into the real estate lady at the house a few days ago," he adds, getting us off the subject.

"What were you doing at the house?" I ask curiously.

"You left in a hurry. I wanted to check to make sure the power got turned back on and everything was all right."

"Was everything okay?"

"It was. Your agent mentioned there's a lot of work to be done before you can list the house."

"Mmhmm. She told me the same. I told her to sell it *as is*."

"I still can't talk you out of selling and coming home?"

"France is my home now. Can we talk about something else?"

"What about the stuff in the house?"

I sigh. I guess not. "I'm going to hire someone to pack it all up and put it in storage until I can arrange to have it shipped here."

"Sounds like a good job for Caleb."

I smile, remembering the day he ran up the driveway juggling weeks' worth of mail. "You really like that boy, don't you?"

"Well, his father is a good man. He's worked with us since we started. He stuck with us through the first year, when there were more bills than work, and we had to pass out IOUs for a few weeks' pay. Caleb, well...he's trying, but he's gotten himself in with a bad crowd and started getting into trouble and missing school. We're just trying to keep him busy and hoping that he grows out of whatever infatuation he has with those other boys."

"That's good of you."

"Well, my mom used to say there are no bad kids, just bad behaviours."

French wine seems to have spurred my curiosity and loosened the reins on my mouth. "Has she been gone long?"

"Several years."

"How'd she die?"

"Breast cancer. We watched her suffer in pain for nearly two years as she died a very slow death. Be thankful that your grandfather spared you that."

"I'm sorry, Ben."

"That's when we moved to the farm we're at now. We used to be on the other side of the highway in Grey county, but Dad couldn't stand living in the house we grew up in after she passed."

"That's how I was feeling when I was home."

"I understand that. Just so you know, there isn't a day go by he doesn't regret that decision. Now he misses the memories they made there and the connection to her."

"Ben, I...."

"Come home, Cora," he pleads. "You'll regret it if you don't. I know there's a lot of work to be done."

"It's not just that," I argue. "That house holds a lot of secrets I don't think I want the answers to." I wipe a tear from my eye.

"It's your history. It's your *home*. Once a country girl, always a country girl." He pauses. "Jake misses you," he adds.

I let out a small laugh.

"What about my career? My promotion? I should just quit and walk away?"

"Yes."

"Oh, okay. So then how would I pay the bills? Property taxes and utility bills come every month, regardless if I'm working or not. The house might be paid for, but there's lots of other debt, and the interest alone on that is killing me right now."

"You'll figure it out."

Now he's starting to frustrate the hell out of me. "Oh, sure. It's that easy is it? All those years of farming didn't help my grandfather keep on top of things."

"You mean to tell me, you went all the way to France for a fancy, expensive education and you can't figure out a way to use it to make money here?"

I growl. "Really? Is your father making money at farming?"

"You know he's not, Cora. That's why Jake and I moved back in with him. To help out. We have a small family business on the side that helps pay the bills. The farming is just something to keep Dad busy and make him feel like he's still useful. He loves working the land."

"You're incredibly frustrating sometimes. I don't want to talk about it anymore."

"So why did you call me then?"

"Because I wanted to share the great news about my promotion and talk about my career. Not about throwing it all away to move home and be miserable."

"I see. Well then, congratulations again. I wish you success and happiness there in France."

"Thanks," I say, feeling disappointed now.

"You take care and keep in touch."

"Say hello to Jake and your dad for me."

"Will do. Can I ask how you got my number?"

I hesitate, trying to think of a lie but come up empty. "Jake gave it to me." I hear a loud thud and someone in the background shout out in pain. "Ben? Is everything okay?"

"Yep, just fine."

"I'll let you go. It was nice to hear your voice."

I hold the phone to my ear, long after he's hung up, replaying the conversation in my mind and wonder what would happen between us if I stayed in Mono Mills. I don't think he and I will ever see eye to eye on a lot of things, but there is an attraction there we both seem to be avoiding. I turn on the television and finish my glass of wine. I'm no longer in a celebratory mood. I don't know why I let Ben get into my head. I look to the heavens for direction. "Pops, if you can hear me, I need your help. What should I do?" My eyes feel heavy and I drift off sitting on the couch, waiting for a sign from the afterlife.

The sun feels warm on my face as I walk over to the old oak tree. Taking a seat beneath it, I lean against the massive trunk and open my book to finish my homework. The leaves provide a cool spot to escape from the unusually hot June. I can hear the rumbling of the headwaters where the rivers merge after their journey through the rugged hills. My grandparents wander out of the house and sit in their usual spots on the front porch. It's their routine: chores, dinner, coffee, and family time. I close my books and put them back in my bag. When I arrive at the porch, Pops has already set up the checkerboard.

"Are you prepared to lose tonight?" he teases. "Winner gets the loser's dessert."

I smile. "Those are some pretty big stakes."

"Nana has made a strawberry shortcake and I'm feeling lucky."

"You don't need two desserts," Nana scolds. "You can barely button your shirt now."

Pops makes a wounded face and looks down at his bulging buttons.

"Don't worry, Nana. He always lets me win anyway."

"Now wait a minute, you think I let you win?" he protests.

"Every time we play," I laugh.

"I would never," he says defensively, trying not to smile.

"Mmhmm. Okay. You go first."

"Did my momma like to play checkers?" I ask, working the conversation up to something that's been on my mind.

Pops slides his checker diagonally into a new spot. "She sure did. She always won as well."

I anticipate his strategy and change direction. "Pops, do you ever think about travelling to new places?"

"Not really. This old house is where I belong."

"You never wonder what it's like in other parts of the world?"

"Nope. Everything I need is right here. All I need in life is my family, friends, and my farm. If I've got those things, I'm a happy man."

"Don't forget food," Nana adds, as she untangles her yarn and rolls it into a ball. "You don't miss too many meals."

I burst out laughing.

"Stick to your knitting, woman," Pops says in jest as he makes a move that guarantees me the win. "Does this have something to do with this trip to France with your school? I saw the permission forms on the table."

"Can I go, Pops? It looked kind of expensive."

He smiles and looks over at Nana, who glances up from her knitting. "Of course, you can go. That's a lot of eggs, but we'll find a way to pay for it."

"I want to travel and see the whole world," I announce.

"Well, when you do, just remember…it doesn't matter where your journey takes you, you can always find your way home. You just need to follow the signs."

As I finish the game, he looks up at me pretending to be shocked. "Now how did that happen? I thought I had ya this time."

I open my eyes and look around the room, expecting to find my grandparents there. I feel a strange energy as I get ready for work. Like someone is watching me.

It looks like it's going to rain, so I open the closet door to get my umbrella. The box from Etienne begins to slide off the shelf and I reach for it, trying to ease it back into place, but there are too many things in the way. As I struggle, it tips farther, and the flap opens, allowing something to go crashing to the floor. I curse as I shove the box forcefully and make sure it stays. I hold my breath for several seconds as I look down at the checkers scattered all over the floor around me. Now that's a little freaky. I glance at the time: I'll have to clean this up later.

I move quickly and manage to get on the 8:15 train. I make my way downtown, as I do every day, but today I'm very aware of my surroundings. Most days, I find a seat and get out my phone to busy myself with emails or catch up on my shows. Today I watch out the window as the scenery passes in a grey drizzly blur of cement and brick. People mindlessly get on and off at every stop. They could be cast members of *The Walking Dead* for all the cheerful energy they project.

I put in my earphones and launch my radio app. I scroll through my favourites and select the Dufferin county country station. Judging from the unimpressed look I get from the gentleman on my left, it's too loud. I turn it down, sit back in my seat, and close my eyes, allowing the familiar song about *going home* soothe me. I don't make any connection between the song playing and my dream last night, not even after I reach into my pocket for my lip gloss and smooth it across my lips. I put the lid back on and turn it sideways to read the label. Strawberry Shortcake.

I'm a little nervous to see what my day will bring. I read through the files regarding the needs of my newest client. I've never handled marketing for a billion-dollar oil and gas company, but their current campaign is to discover new talent to work in their industry. That, I can help with. I'm continually interrupted by emails from my persistent real estate agent. I hold my head and growl in frustration. I'm never going to be able to concentrate on this new project until all these loose ends in Canada are tied up.

My door opens and a young boy from the mailroom enters, pushing a trolley stacked with several boxes marked fragile.

"What's that?" I ask.

"I don't know," he admits as he moves the top carton onto my desk.

I stand and look at the delivery label. "Wait a minute. I'm not working on the agricultural farm project anymore."

"Your name is on the delivery," he says, as he unloads the rest of the cartons and stacks them on the floor.

"Yes, but someone else is looking after that account now."

He nods as he backs out of the room. "I just deliver stuff where I'm told. Have a great day."

Fiona emails me details on a company that will pack up my grandparents' belongings and discard anything that's not of value. I have a moment of anxiety over it. I don't know what's of value and what's not. Judging from the quote she's provided for a sea container, having it all sent here is out of the question.

One of my coworkers glances into my office on her way past. "Oooh, what's in the boxes?" she pauses and asks.

"I have no idea," I say, getting to my feet. She watches as I poke my pen through the tape and then pull open one of the flaps.

"What is it?" she asks in anticipation.

I open my eyes wide and then wrinkle my nose. "Eggs." I move to the stack of cartons beside my desk.

"And?" she asks, walking farther into the room as I open the next one.

I shrug. "More eggs." I carefully move the cartons one by one, opening them as I go.

"That's a LOT of omelettes," she says, as she turns to leave. "Could have been worse, they could have sent you live chickens."

I sit pensively on the edge of my desk and then it hits me. *You can always find your way home, just follow the signs.* I asked Pops for help and he sent me signs.

I move at a quick pace down the hall and hope my boss is in her office. I knock on the partially closed door and peek in.

"Cora, come in. What can I do for you?"

I take a deep breath and begin, before I second-guess my decision. "Marion, I want to thank you for trusting me with the Ultron Petroleum account, but I have to turn it down."

She raises her brows. "May I ask why?"

I place my hand on my chest, trying to slow my rapidly beating heart. "I have to go back home. I had no idea there was so much involved in dealing with the estate, and I can't concentrate on this project while I'm stressing over all the things that need my attention there. I need to pack up my grandmother's family heirlooms and donate all my pops' clothes, and sell the farm," I ramble.

"I see."

"I don't want to disappoint you by doing a half-assed job on such an important account."

She studies me for a long while and I begin to wonder if I've just effectively talked myself out of a job all together.

She leans back against her desk and smiles. "What's his name?"

"Ben," I reply without thinking. A look of confusion morphs across my face. Why did I just say that?

"I like your work, Cora."

"Thank you," I brace myself for the *but*.

"Is there internet service on your farm?"

"Yes, ma'am. Slower than dial-up most days, but there is service."

She gets to her feet and walks toward the door; I follow. "Go home and tend to your business. Get the guy. Take your laptop and work from there, you can schedule conference calls with the team."

"Seriously?" I ask, feeling very grateful.

"Seriously."

"How can I thank you?"

"You can create me a fantastic campaign that they're going to love, and you'll be back in three weeks to pitch it to them in person."

She senses my split second of doubt. "You've got this," she says confidently.

I smile. "I do."

CHAPTER NINE

This time I withhold my tip until the driver helps me get my trunk out of the car. He moves it a few feet to the edge of the walkway before getting back into the driver's seat and driving away. At least this time it's not raining. It would be wonderful if I returned home to find the house looking exactly the way I remember it when I was a young girl. Would anybody blame me for wishing the past several weeks were all just a dream?

At least I don't have to try and balance on an old tin bucket to get in the front door any longer. I think of Ben, and his distracting mass of muscles, as I climb the new steps to the front door. I didn't tell him I was coming home. I'm not even sure if I should have come back, but deep down I know why I did. Answers. And not just about my family.

Besides, Ben would pressure me to know my intention for the farm, and I don't want to tell him that I haven't changed my mind about selling; yet. I curse as I drag the awkward trunk into the house, threatening to ensure it's the first thing to go up for auction. After I settle in, I walk down the driveway and grab what's in the mailbox. The sun is warm, and the old oak tree where I used to read invites me into its shade for old times' sake. A slight breeze rustles the leaves, making them sing me an old familiar song as I flip through the flyers, before tossing them aside. The local newspaper blows open to the community events page and something catches my eye. 'Dufferin County Home Show.' I read the ad for the event that's happening today, which promises many vendors specializing in home renovations, repairs, and decorating. That's what I need.

I get in the car and make the short trip down to the next road. Surely, I'll be able to find the proper trades people who can help me get this place in tip-top shape before it goes on the market.

The agricultural building at the fairgrounds is humming with activity. I haven't been here since I was a girl and Pops had entered some of his livestock in a competition at the fall fair. I wander up and down the aisles, collecting brochures and requesting estimates. I'm waiting to talk to one of the landscape companies when I overhear a familiar voice that makes my heart flutter. Only a few steps down the next aisle, I see him and get a nervous kind of angst in the pit of my stomach. I'm not ready to face him yet, so I'm going to try and get past without him noticing while he's busy with a potential client.

"Cora!"

I feel tension wind tightly in my muscles.

"I didn't know you were back."

I fake a smile. "Hi, Jake, I didn't hear you sneak up behind me."

He wrinkles his brow, and glances at all the commotion around us. "I wasn't exactly sneaking."

I laugh. "What are you doing here?"

He nods in the direction of the booth I was trying to avoid. "This is my brother's business; it might be hard to believe, but he's an architectural expert. He gave it up..." He catches himself. "It's not important why he gave it up, but my mother begged him to get back to doing what he loved before she died"

"Makes sense. You guys know how to do everything."

"Ben is the restoration expert, I'm more of a 'salvage what you can and make something new' kind of guy. Either way, it helps pay the bills." He glows with pride. "What are you doing here?" He looks down at the stack of brochures in my hand. "Oh, of course. You need work done at the house."

I nod. Ben finishes with his customer and wanders over. "Hello, Cora."

"Hi, Ben."

Feeling awkward, I try to avoid eye contact with him. I begin to flip through a book of photos on the table of the work they've done. I stop at the picture of Gordon Henderson's law firm and let out a small laugh. "Now it all makes sense," I say beneath my breath.

"What does?" Jake asks curiously.

I blush, ashamed I said it loud enough for him to hear. I glance over at Ben. "The secretary said that the renovation specialist they hired was an annoying perfectionist."

Jake starts to laugh. Ben's body stiffens and his chest puffs out, as if he's had to take a deep breath to restrain his thoughts. He scruffs his beard. "Is that so?"

"It is," I confirm.

"She didn't seem to have any complaints when I was there. In fact, she was kind of sweet on me. She brought me coffee and donuts every day."

"Probably thinking if you were eating, you wouldn't be talking."

Jake intervenes. "If you're looking to hire someone to restore that old farmhouse of yours, you'll find nobody better than Ben." He glances at another potential customer at the table and excuses himself. "I'll be right back."

"That depends," Ben says, staring at me. "Are you staying or selling, Miss Scott?"

I start to feel my blood boil. If that's the way he wants to play it, two can play the same game.

"I'm selling, Mr..." I glance over his shoulder at the name on the company banner. 'Dover Construction.' My current rant comes to a complete stop. His name is Ben Dover? "You have got to be kidding me?" I ask.

"About what?"

"Is this a joke?"

"I don't know what you're talking about."

A small ghost of a smug grin curls on his lips, and I know he's just playing stupid. I refuse to say it out loud.

"Well then," Jake says as he returns. "Do you want to give me a list of things you want done, and I'll write you up a quote? Of course, you'll get the special friends and family discount."

Ben and I are still engaged in a power struggle. Jake furrows his brow and looks between us nervously. "Cora?"

I snap out of it. "No thanks, Jake. I think I've made my decision."

"I assure you, if you want good quality work, we're the best restoration experts out there. And we have a vested interest in you and your property."

"I'm going to do the work myself," I blurt out. What the ever-loving-hell did I just say? Jake looks shocked.

"Are you now?" Ben says, bursting out into laughter and aggravating me even further.

"Yes. I've just decided that I'll do this project on my own."

"Cora, that's a lot of work," Jake starts to reason.

"Oh no, brother. Obviously, Cora knows what she's doing, and she's made her decision. She doesn't strike me as the kind of person to change her mind."

"No, I'm not," I confirm.

Jake shakes his head in disbelief. "All right then. Good luck with your project."

I walk away with my head held high and proud that I didn't let *Ben Dover* get the best of me. I close the car door and turn the key, then reality suddenly sets in. I close my eyes and pray for help as I lower my head, repeatedly banging it on the steering wheel.

On the way up the driveway, I try to take note of all the things that need to be tended to and feel very overwhelmed. "What was it that Pops used to say?" I murmur. "*Don't ever put limits on yourself. You can do anything you want to do. Never stop trying.*" Something like that.

I lie awake thinking about my mother. There are so many questions I'd like to ask her. So many unanswered questions surrounding her death. What about my father? Who was he? Did he know about me? I get to my feet and walk down what feels like a never-ending hallway. I stand on the outside of the door, hesitating. I don't know why I'm afraid to go in, but I feel like I'm about to have a panic attack standing here with my hand on the doorknob. I push the door open, and I'm teleported nearly thirty years back in time. Not a thing has changed. It's exactly the way my mother left it. I sit on the side of the bed and turn on the bedside lamp. I pick up the stuffed dog that's sitting beside me on the bed and cuddle it to my chest. "Why? Momma, I just want to know why you left me." I lift my feet and lay back on the bed. In just a few moments I'm asleep.

The next morning is a miserable one, cloudy and drizzly just enough that it stunts progress of anything to be done outside. I light the wood stove and add just enough wood to take the dampness out of the room. The smell and the crackling have a very relaxing effect on me, but I better get some work done. I unfold one of the boxes I've collected from the grocery store and heavily tape the bottom to secure it. Glancing around the room, I search for things I can start to pack. I'm at a loss. Everything has either sentimental value or is something that looks like it has some age to it, and I'm uncertain what, if anything, is a family heirloom. I'll call Lynn later and check on Aunt Bea's health. Maybe there's a chance she can come out and go through some of this stuff with me. On to the next project then. I grab a handful of garbage bags and walk down the hall to Pops' room. It has an off-putting smell of antiseptic and something else. Death? I gather up Pops' clothing and take them into the second-floor bathroom they had renovated to accommodate an apartment-size washer and dryer, when Nanas couldn't handle carrying heavy baskets up and down the steps anymore. If I'm going to donate these clothes, I should at least try to wash the musty farm smell out of them.

I'm only one step into the bathroom when I find myself with a wet sock. I drop the clothing on the floor and turn on the light. A slow trickle of water, starting from the base of the toilet, makes its way across the floor following the grout line in the tile. "Great! Now what?"

I look out the window to see if the rain has stopped. It looks like I'm heading into the local hardware store. I open my email as I walk to my car and read a list of things to buy from my fiery five foot Irish real estate agent. She's busting my ass with a list a mile long of things that need to be done to get this house on the market. If I have to go into town, I might as well get the supplies I think I'm going to need to do these projects on my own.

I wander up and down the aisles of the huge hardware conglomerate that popped up after I left for Europe. I'm completely lost. After placing a few cans of door and trim paint into the cart, I check my list.

"Where do I find trim?" I ask the girl at the paint desk.

"Aisle eighteen," she answers without looking up.

Typical big box store. I miss my small-town, family-owned hardware store. It's a shame that stores like this force them out of business. I didn't realize that trim came in so many thicknesses, styles, or lengths. Primed or not-primed. I grab one and hope for the best. On the way to the check out, I pass the aisle that says 'Plumbing & Plumbing Repairs'. I almost forgot that I have to deal with that leaking toilet before I have to replace the floor. I walk up the aisle confounded by the well-stocked shelves. Who knew that a toilet had so many parts? I take them, one at a time off the pegs and read the packages, trying to figure out which part I need. A store assistant comes around the corner, and when I establish eye contact and begin to ask him a question, he quickly turns and goes the other direction, pretending not to see me. I mumble under my breath as I begin to take one of each part and toss them in my cart. I hear someone behind me intentionally clear their throat, and I turn quickly at the familiar sound.

"Fuck me," I say aloud.

Ben laughs.

"What are you doing here?" I ask, as I take a long look at him in his faded jeans and leather tool belt.

He holds up a pipe fitting and plumbing solder. "Working on a house on Church Street. What are you doing here?" He peers over the edge of my cart and raises his brow. "Rebuilding the latrine from the ground up?"

I sigh. "The stupid toilet is leaking."

"Ah." He takes all the parts out of my cart, stacks them on a shelf, then reaches up and grabs a wax seal. "This is what you need," he says, as he tosses it into my cart.

As much as it pains me to be nice to him when he's being assholey, I do appreciate his help. "Thank you."

He nods. "What's the trim for?"

I hesitate, not sure if I want to engage him in further conversation. Doing so will likely open myself up for more ridicule. "It's for around one of the windows."

He takes it out of the cart. "This is too wide for a window." He walks, and I follow. He pulls a length off the shelf and checks to make sure it's not warped. "Here, this matches the trim on your windows."

I shrug. "How do you know that?"

"I notice things. It's my job. Do you have a miter saw?"

"A what?" I look at him like a deer in the headlights.

"The tool to cut the angles with?"

"Oh. I'm sure there's one somewhere in the barn."

"Have you ever done this before?"

I shift my weight to one side, growing tired of the inquisition. "Obviously not."

He scratches his beard, pensively, and I prepare for the censure. "Which window is it?"

"The front window in the hall that faces north."

"That window is rotten, Cora. I noticed it when I was putting up the front steps. There's a leak in eavestrough and the rain and runoff from the ice has been running straight down the side of the wall and sitting in the ledge. Since it faces north it barely gets any sun to help it dry. Putting a new piece of decorative trim on it won't help. The entire window and framing needs to be replaced, and the eavestrough as well."

I see dollar signs and I don't like it. "I thought if I just prettied it up some, it would look better when I list it."

"Well, yes. But anybody spending money on a house is going to do a building inspection. They're going to discover the rot underneath and think you tried to hide it."

Now I feel stressed and Ben can sense it.

"Look, why don't you let me come by and fix it?"

"I can do it myself..."

He holds up his hand, stopping me. "No charge. I just want to help."

Why do I always feel suspicious when people offer to help me? I think on it a moment. "Okay, this one is way over my head," I admit.

He slides the trim back on the shelf. "I'll stop by when I'm finished this job and see what we need."

We walk toward the check out and I get in a different line, feeling like I just need to put some space between us.

"Just leave that toilet repair, I'll look after that when I'm there as well," he says as he walks past me on his way out.

The cashier bats her eyelashes at him. "Hey, Ben."

"Hey, Debbie." He stops to chat with her and leans against the counter.

"Feel free to put me on the top of your *to-do* list," she says flirtatiously.

I feel my face flush as she focuses on Ben and hands me my bag without even looking at me.

He smiles. "Now, the last I heard you were going out with Jason."

"We broke up, last week."

"Well, he's a very stupid man to let you get away."

She giggles and twists her hair around her finger.

"Excuse me," I say as I shoulder past him.

"I'll see you later this afternoon," he says, looking amused.

I roll my eyes. "Whenever you can squeeze me in on your *to-do* list." He chuckles as I walk away.

A few hours later, I'm on a ladder with a straw broom trying to knock down some of the cobwebs and dislodge a few birdhouses when he arrives with his brother.

"You be careful up there," Jake hollers, as he gets out of the truck.

"I'm fine," I insist.

Ben walks over and presses firmly on the metal stays and locks the ladder in the open position. "You know they work better when you lock em properly, right?"

I can hear Jake chuckle from a few feet away. "The window is over there," I say pointing to my left. Ben smirks and wanders over to where his brother is already assessing the rot.

When I'm finished with the cobwebs, I climb down and start to sweep the drying mud of the walkway. Ben glances over to see what I'm doing. "Aunt Bea is feeling better. She's coming to visit tomorrow."

"Well, that's good to hear. You want the bad news?"

"Not really, but you're going to tell my anyway."

"Jake and I agree. We need to remove this window and replace all the rotten frame. And the window too. We won't know just how bad the rot is, and how much of the wall is affected, until we get in there."

He must read the panic on my face and answers my unasked question. "We'll just put the materials on our business credit account and keep track of what we use. You can pay us a little at a time when you have the money."

I'm speechless for a moment.

"What?" he asks suspiciously at my silence.

"Nothing. Thank you. Sometimes I wonder if you two are for real. I've never met anyone like you before."

"You should really spend more time here, we're all good folk."

"Touché." He just can't resist taking a jab at me.

He flashes me a boyish smile and I find myself drawn in by a charm that he normally keeps hidden.

"We'll start in the morning."

"See you then."

"I like my eggs, over easy."

"Make sure you tell the waitress at Angel's Diner."

He grins. "I like my girls feisty."

I open the door to the house and give him a mischievous grin. "Then don't leave her a good tip." The screen door snaps shut behind me as I step inside.

CHAPTER TEN

Ben wasn't joking. They get started at the crack of dawn. The constant hammering is starting to annoy me. I pile a few more relics on the table and take a quick look at the progress being made on the hole in the side of my house. The longer he's here, the more money it's going to cost me. At least, that's the excuse I'm telling myself for wanting him to be gone.

The unmistakable hum of a car coming up the dirt road alerts me to the fact that Aunt Bea is here. Before I can get on my shoes and get out the door, Ben and his brother are helping her out of the car. For someone who normally has the patience of a gnat, Ben exercises great tolerance for Aunt Bea's laboured stroll. With strong arms beside her, she manages the new porch steps with ease. Ben glances up at me and I give him the acknowledgement he's looking for. He was right. As much as it pains me to admit it, he's been right about everything so far.

"Won't your friend be joining us?" I ask, curious as to why her personal support worker isn't getting out of the car. I return her polite wave.

"No, dear. She's going to run some errands in town and come back for me later."

Once she's safely in the house, the boys take their leave and return to their current project. "Such lovely boys," Aunt Bea notes.

I watch as they go back to their power tools. "They are," I admit. My eyes stay locked on Ben as he picks up the sledge hammer and knocks through the existing framed window with a powerful blow. For the first time, he's so focused on his task that he doesn't notice me watching. There's such beauty in his strength and muscular conformation, I can't tear my gaze away. It's a shame he always has to open his mouth and ruin it all.

I help Aunt Bea sit at the kitchen table and pour her a cup of tea that I've made in my nana's 'Brown Betty' teapot. She smiles. "I gave this tea pot to Maggie and Bill as a wedding gift."

"Oh, I didn't know that." It makes me happy to uncover a little bit of my elusive family history. "I'll add this to the list of family heirlooms that I will take with me back to Europe."

"Maggie's father didn't want her to marry my brother."

I raise my brow. "No?"

"No. Her father wanted her to marry someone who could provide better for her. A banker or an obstetrician." She takes a sip of tea. "People were always having babies. Like they had nothing else to do."

"I guess the winters were long and cold back in those days," I laugh.

She rolls he eyes. "They should have taken up a hobby. Like knitting. That's what I did."

I put a bowl of soup in front of her and hand her a spoon. "Chicken noodle. I hope that's okay?"

"That's my favourite."

I sigh relief. In the centre of the table I place a plate of assorted sandwiches. I figure the best option is to let her pick what she likes. Of course, she immediately picks through them and takes the ham. I guess we're going to have a gassy afternoon. I try not to laugh. "Did you ever get married?"

"No."

"You never found that *special* guy?"

"I did."

"Oh...do tell."

"His name was James Cooper. Jimmy. He was my high school sweetheart."

Why does that name sound familiar? "This sounds steamy. What happened? Why didn't you get married?"

"We were young and foolish. He promised me the world, but he went off to college and met another girl there."

"Oh," I frown, feeling disappointed. "And you never found anyone else to share your life with?"

"Never tried," she admits between mouthfuls of soup. "He was my one true love. He found his way back home a few years ago. Came knocking on my door."

"He did?"

"What did he want?"

She scowls at me. "He wanted me, of course. He said he never stopped loving me after all those years."

"That's so romantic. Where is he now?"

"He passed away last year."

"Oh, I'm sorry."

"Don't be, we had two wonderful years together before he died. It took many years for him to come back to me, but the heart wants what it wants."

Her words strike home, and I begin to feel a heaviness in my chest as I glance out the window at Ben.

I begin to clear the uneaten sandwiches off the table and wonder what I was thinking. "There's enough food here for an army," I say aloud.

"Did I hear someone say food?" Jake asks as he enters the kitchen. "Sorry for intruding, I wondered if I could fill my water bottle."

"Yes, of course. Please help yourself to something to eat."

"Thank you. I'm starving." He removes his hat and washes his hands in the kitchen sink. "I'll let Ben know *after* I've had my fill."

"Good plan."

"The man loves his sandwiches," he jokes.

"Good to know he's capable of love." I feel my face turn red with shame when I realize I just said that aloud.

Jake narrows his eyes at me.

I quickly get off that topic. "Aunt Bea, if you've had enough to eat, I have some things put aside that I'm hoping you can tell me about."

"Like what?"

I have a feeling I'm about to get a good talking to from Jake and I'd rather avoid it. "Let's go into the living room where you'll be more comfortable." I help her into the other room and smile as she chooses my pops' chair.

"There's a small watercolour painting of the house hanging in the hallway. For some reason I have a feeling it's important."

"Bring it to me, let me see it."

I retrieve it, and as I return to the room, her face lights up and then a look of sorrow takes over. I'm confused. She lifts a shaking hand and takes it from me, pausing for a very long time before she speaks. "Your mother painted this picture," she finally says.

Now I understand her reaction. I, myself, just felt a moment of excitement followed by sadness. I watch as she gently brushes her fingers across the canvas, having what seems to be a nostalgic moment.

I study the butterflies that are painted in the garden with meticulous detail. "I should have known it was one of hers." I stare at it, hoping every line and every brush stroke might somehow help connect me with my mother.

"She had a fascination with monarch butterflies," Aunt Bea recalls, as she turns the picture over and dusts off the frame, exposing a signature and date. "She was only just thirteen when she painted this picture. She was so talented. She could see beauty in a sea of ugliness. It was such a shame, what happened."

I feel a nervous energy begin to run through my body. "Aunt Bea. What happened to my mother?"

"She was just a child herself when you were born."

I nod, "Yes, she was only sixteen." There's a long pensive pause, but I can't wait any longer. "How did she die?"

Her eyes glaze over with a heart-wrenching mournfulness. "Your grandmother had a chest at the end of her bed."

"Yes, but it's locked, and I can't find the key."

"The key is taped to the bottom of the drawer of her jewelry box. Go get it and bring me the scrapbook with the orange cover."

I hurry, like a child on a treasure hunt, and return a few minutes later with the book. I feel a slight nervous tremble in my hand as I sit down beside her and open the cover.

"Maggie kept this scrapbook, so she had memories of all the good times with your momma."

I furrow a brow. "I take it there were a lot of bad times, then?"

She flips through the first few pages of birth announcements and baby photos. "She was such a happy baby. It's a miracle that she was ever born."

"Oh? Why is that?"

"We didn't have fancy hospitals or machinery like nowadays. Back then, you often didn't know what went wrong, or why."

I flip through the next few pictures of my mother's first birthday and her first haircut.

"Maggie had a hard time carrying babies. Lost a few. It was hard on them both. When that little girl, *your mother*, was born healthy, I saw a joy in my brother's eyes that I'd never forget. Then a time came when I thought I'd never see joy in his eyes again."

A feeling of distress comes over me. "Nana never talked about my mom. Pops said it made her heart sad." I place my hand on top of hers. "Please tell me what happened."

"Everyone was shocked when she came home one afternoon, at the age of fifteen, and announced she was with child." She looks up at me and gives me a sympathetic smile. "It wasn't something that was considered *acceptable* in the community thirty-two years ago, but there was never EVER any doubt that you would be born."

Her comment alarms me. I had never considered that my existence was a decision made by a fifteen-year-old girl. "Yes, but how did she die?" I ask anxiously.

"Your momma suffered a terrible sadness," she adds after a few moments of contemplation. "Your grandparents did everything they could to get her some help."

"What are you saying? She suffered from depression?"

"Yes. Poor thing. Misery took her down a dark path."

Dark path? I continue to flip through the pictures of my mother as a young girl. She looked happy. My grandparents looked happy. What could have happened that was so horrible it pulled this smiling child into a darkness that completely shattered my family? Was it my fault?

"I was almost three when she died. I don't remember much about what was going on. I remember her as a happy and loving mother." I feel myself becoming emotional. "I miss her."

"I'm glad that's how you remember her. It was hard on Bill and Maggie, watching their daughter deteriorate and not being able to help."

"Depression isn't fatal."

Her eyes glaze over as she turns the pages to the very end of the bound, orange book.

As morbid as it seems to have included a death certificate in a scrapbook of memories, I'm glad it's there. I read through the legal details. "Allison Grace Scott; deceased 1991." I'm not sure I want to continue reading.

"Go on," she encourages. "The truth is there in black and white."

I take in a long slow breath.

"The coroner's report should be on the next page."

Reluctantly I turn the page and begin to read. The toxicology report shows excessive amounts of anti-depressants in her system. "Cause of death...Suicide." I read aloud. My blood runs cold as I try to process it.

"It was a terrible, terrible time," Aunt Bea recollects.

Overwhelmed I get to my feet. "Where are my manners? I'll get you another tea." I move quickly to the kitchen, unsuccessfully fighting back the tears. When I turn the corner, I find Ben standing in the middle of the room. I stop dead in my tracks. "You startled me."

"I didn't mean to." He nods his head toward the empty lunch plate. "Jake said there was food."

I wipe the dampness from my cheeks. "I didn't hear you come in. How long have you been in here?"

There's an awkward moment between us when our eyes lock and I know he's heard it all. "Excuse me." I brush past him to get the sugar for Aunt Bea's tea. I expect him to back up and get out of my way. That's what any decent person would do, but not Ben. He holds his ground, leaving minimal personal space between us. I can feel the warmth of his breath on my neck.

"Cora, I'm sorry."

His strong hand firmly grips my shoulder, offering his condolence. I close my eyes and find the strength to keep myself from collapsing into his arms. There's nothing I need more, right now, than to fall against his firm muscular chest and allow him to wrap me in his protective arms. I know I shouldn't want that, but I do. A few stuttered breaths and a sudden burst of restraint allows me to cope. "It's okay." I turn to face him. "I wanted to know...I *needed* to know."

"It's okay to be upset," he assures me as he reaches for me. I slip from his grasp and pick up the teacup. "I should take Aunt Bea her tea before it gets cold."

His jaw tightens, and frustration darkens his eyes as he nods and stands aside.

As I place the tea on the table beside her, I hear the front door screen bang shut.

I purse my lips and try to smile but fail. Aunt Bea reaches out and takes my hand. "You were loved, child. No matter what you may be thinking right now, your mother loved you. She was a broken girl. There was nothing anyone could do to make things right. Your grandparents tried to shelter you from the truth. I'm not going to say it was the right thing to do, but it was their choice. They wanted you to grow up knowing love, nothing else."

I give her hand a little squeeze. "Thank you, for telling me the truth."

"It was time."

The door opens and in walks Aunt Bea's personal support worker.

"It's about time you got back here. It's past my lunchtime," Aunt Bea scolds.

Lynn looks at me confused and I jump to her aid. "Aunt Bea. You just finished eating lunch."

"What?"

"You just finished eating a bowl of soup and a sandwich," I remind her.

A sly grin curls on her lips. "I know, I'm just messing with her. Keeps her on her toes."

I extend my hand and help her to her feet. "You need to be nicer to her," I whisper. "Looking after us Scott women is not an easy task. We're kind of stubborn."

"Eh," she scoffs.

I laugh once. "Aunt Bea. I'm wondering...do you have any idea who my father was?"

"I remember a boy named Eddie or Robbie. I get confused sometimes."

I give her a half-smile. "That's okay, don't worry about it."

"It might say on the original copy of your birth certificate."

"My birth certificate? I haven't come across that yet."

"Maggie never threw anything away. She used to hide stuff in the strangest places. After she passed away, we found two brand-new one hundred-dollar bills in a pair of shoes in her closet. That reminds me, I should go through everything she gave me before she passed away and make sure there's nothing hidden in anything. You should be careful with what you're giving away. It wouldn't surprise me if your mother did the same thing.

"I'll keep my eyes open," I promise.

"Give me a hug and make it a good one. It could be the last one."

I wrap my arms around her and give her a tight squeeze. "Don't say things like that."

"I'm not gonna live forever, you know. I'm at the age where every day above ground is a good one. Until the day I get to be with my beloved James, again."

I suddenly realize why that name sounds familiar. It's the name on the tombstone, on the grave that used to belong to Pops. He gave up his spot beside Nana, so his sister could rest beside the love of her life for all eternity. My heart beats a little happier knowing.

Jake is waiting at the steps to help Aunt Bea to the car. I glance past them to look for Ben and find him violently pounding the hell out of something with a hammer. He means business; his jaw clenched tight, and a thick beading of sweat dots his brow.

"Jake, I think it's time to call it a day. I need some peace and quiet and time to think," I say.

He nods his acknowledgement.

As I open the door, I hear the sound of tools and scraps of wood being tossed into the back of the truck. Before long, tires spin in the dirt as they depart with excessive speed. I lift a stack of papers out of the chest and carry them out to the living room to sort. Page by page, document by document I skim through them. Aunt Bea was right; my nana didn't throw anything out.

I'm not sure how long I've been sitting here, but I suddenly notice that the sun has gone down. There's a damp chill in the air tonight. I begin to feel like every dusty corner of this house is hiding secrets.

When I first arrived back home, I felt my nana's presence here. It was almost comforting. Tonight, I feel alone. The walls begin to close in around me. My imagination gets the best of me. I need to get out of here, there are too many secrets, too many memories. I can't breathe.

CHAPTER ELEVEN

I find myself in town at one of the local eateries. I don't feel much like food, so I hoist myself up into one of the tall chairs in the bar and order a drink. And then another.

"Drinking alone?"

I close my eyes and sigh. I just can't get away from these guys. I glance to my left. "Hi, Jake. Are you and your brother stalking me?"

"This is our Saturday night hang-out, so it would appear it's you that's stalking us."

I swirl the ice in the bottom of my glass. "Of all the gin joints, in all the towns," I say as I lift it to my lips.

He smirks. "We're sitting at our usual table over in the corner, if you want to join us."

I lean back in my chair and look past him. Ben is engaged in conversation with someone at the table and bursts out laughing at something that was said. Even from across the room, I can see his dimples when he smiles.

"Thanks anyway. I'm fine here on my own."

He cocks his head to the side. "What do you think Ben's going to say about that?"

I laugh once. "I don't care what your brother says...or what he thinks, for that matter."

Jake leans in close. "That's not true, and we both know it."

I ignore him and signal the bartender for another drink as he gives up and walks away. The stunning blonde puts a clean glass in front of me. "You know," she says as she tips the bottle and pours. "We're not a high-class establishment here." She gives a discreet nod, directing my attention to the other side of the bar. "Hell, most nights if you've got all your own teeth you're overdressed." A rather sketchy looking dude raises his beer bottle and stares at me. I get a sense that his older, weathered appearance is due to his alcohol consumption and not his actual age. He gives me a crooked smile and I get an uncomfortable feeling, so I look away.

"The McCarthy brothers are about the best men you're gonna find in this town," she continues.

"Who?"

She directs my attention to the table in the corner. "Jake and Ben McCarthy."

"McCarthy?" I wrinkle my nose, feeling confused. "I thought their last name was Dover."

Everyone within earshot laughs and she gives them a warning look. "Did Ben tell you that?" she asks, trying to hide her own amusement.

"No, I...the name of their family business is Dover Construction. I thought..." My face turns red as the chuckling around me continues.

"Don't feel bad, sweetie. You're not the first person he let believe his name is *Ben Dover*."

"That doesn't surprise me," I grumble.

"Apparently, Dover is the name of the county in Ireland where his father was born."

"Of course, it is." I hold my hands over my face, trying to hide my embarrassment. I can't believe I'm that gullible. Suddenly I see the humor in it, and I begin to grin. And then chuckle. By the time I find the bottom of my glass I've had a good laugh at my own expense, and I feel a little less...miserable. It doesn't even bother me that the guy from across the bar has edged his way around and is now sitting beside me. Staring. The whisky is already giving me a buzz, and I'm starting to think that maybe I shouldn't have taken one of Etienne's pills before I left the house.

"Can I buy you another round?" The weathered man, who's lean and small in stature runs his tongue over his gums and waits for an answer.

I can think of a million reasons why this is a bad idea, one of them being that I can feel Ben's stare from across the room, but I accept anyway. As the bartender slides the glass in front of me, she grumbles under her breath so that only I can hear. "No teeth. Just saying."

My pops used to say there's someone for everybody. Surely there is a girl out there for this guy, but it's not me. I'm just being polite, or at least that's what I tell myself. The noise level ramps up on the other side of the room as the game on the TV riles up the boys. I spy an old jukebox in the corner and decide they need a little competition. It isn't until I slide off my chair that I realize just how tipsy I'm starting to get. I flip through the song options and laugh. "Looks like seventies country music it is."

I push the button, but nothing happens. "Crap." I try to walk, without weaving, back to the bar. "Hey, buddy, do you have a quarter? I want to listen to music."

He digs deep into his pocket. "Only if you dance with me."

I stare at his mouth while he talks. Trying to count his teeth. "Meh, why not." I shrug as I try to take the quarter out of his hand.

He smiles and releases it. "Go ahead, darling. Play our song."

The bartender makes a sour face and I try not to laugh. "We haven't played music in this bar in a long time."

"Apparently since the seventies." I empty my glass before I return to the jukebox.

"Let's see. Charlie Pride? Loretta Lynn? Conway Twitty." I get excited. "Oh, OH OH! I got it." I push the button and again, nothing happens. "What the fuck?" I give it a little jiggle.

"Need help?"

The sound of his voice sends a sizzle of electricity through my veins. I hold onto the front of the jukebox to keep from tipping over as I look up at Ben. Damn. When did he get so tall? "Nope. I'm good. You can keep moving along. Nothing to see here."

Ben smirks and crosses his arms. "Oh, really?"

"Yes, really. I've got this." I insist. "I don't need you." The booze starts to fuel my mouth into an uncontrollable rant. "But that's who you are, right? You're the great *Ben Dover*...fixer of everything!"

He rakes his fingers through his hair and chuckles. "All right then. I'll just carry on through to the washroom."

"Thank you," I say exasperated, as I go back to pushing buttons and shaking the jukebox like a pinball machine.

Ben leans down to whisper in my ear. "You might want to plug it in." He winks and gives me a victorious smile as he turns and walks away.

Please tell me he's not right. I look at the vacant wall socket, then over at the plug dangling from the side of the machine and growl. "Know-it-all!" Flashing lights brighten the dark little corner once it's connected to power. Who knew? Apparently, Ben and his sexy tattoos and rugged chiseled muscles; and his lips, under that beard. Oh, Lord. What's wrong with me? I need to put him out of my mind. I pick a happy upbeat tune and turn to find the entire bar staring at me.

My dance partner eagerly awaits and I'm feeling a little inspired. I reach out to take his hand and he pulls me in. I'm not sure who's leading, but it's a struggle to keep some distance between us. It's a battle that makes a three-minute song feel like it's three hours long. Thank goodness it's almost done. I'm thirsty and my buzz is starting to fade.

The pace of this song might be a little too ambitious for me in my liquored-up condition. In some fancy move, I'm flung to the side and spun around and suddenly end up facing the opposite direction. I'm surprised I don't tip over. There's Ben, leaning against the jukebox smiling, with a stack of quarters in his hand. I give him a pleading look, but he shows me no mercy. One by one, he drops them into the machine and selects a bunch of songs.

When the current song ends, the tempo changes. Ben chuckles audibly as he walks away, and his selection of slow music begins to play. Gums Magee pulls me in to his chest and holds me like a boa constrictor. I can't breathe and I can't break away. At just the right height, he sinks his face into my chest and nestles between my boobs. I'm gonna kill Ben McCarthy. The bartender holds up a beer and I nod my head in agreement. I manage to dance us close enough to take it out of her hand. I don't normally mix drinks, but this is a necessary survival decision. I'm surprised at how quickly it evaporates. When the song ends, I excuse myself to use the ladies' room. For a minute I think he's going to follow me in there.

In a quiet moment of reflection, while I'm sitting on the toilet, I realize I've made a mistake and now I've probably created myself a stalker. I wonder if I text the restaurant if they'll do stall service? I'll just hide in here all night. I slowly open the bathroom door and peek out. Luckily, Gums isn't paying attention, so I sneak out and head toward the opposite side of the bar. It puts me next to the McCarthy brothers, but I think it's likely the best option.

I know most of the guys over in this corner; they've been working with Ben on the house.

"Hi, Cora," one of them, named Steve, says loudly as he joins them.

"Shhhh. I'm hiding," I advise.

He gives me a confused look. "What's with the music?" he asks the others.

"Cora felt like dancing tonight," Ben smirks, as he tips his beer to his lips.

"Well then, let's go." Steve holds out his hand. "I haven't danced in years."

I accept, and a look washes over Ben's face. Deep down I hope that look is jealousy. I follow Steve to an open spot by the bar, and we dance in small circles to a mellow tune. Every time I come back around to face where Ben sits, he's watching. Attentively. I think he's regretting pumping the jukebox full of quarters. I've become the most popular girl in the joint. I might even be the *only* girl in the place, since my dance card is now full.

The bartender passes me beers between songs, and I lose track of how many I've had, or who's paying for them. I don't even care who I'm dancing with anymore. The music has carried me back into a reminiscent time that has lots of happy memories for me. I remember sitting on a bale of hay in that drafty barn, listening to Johnny Cash and Loretta Lynn, watching Pops work on the broken-down, old farm truck. How I loved riding in that truck as we bounced around out in the back field, checking on the fences and the crops. I can smell the manure the neighbour used to spread, like I was standing in the middle of the field. I jump back to reality for a moment when I realize that smell is the guy I'm currently dancing with.

My eyes start playing tricks on me, as I try to focus on a figure across the dark crowded room. He looks an awful lot like Etienne. Until he moves out of the shadows, I'm not a hundred percent it's not. Crystal Gayle sings, "Don't It Make My Brown Eyes Blue" and my happy mood comes to a screeching halt. Why would I think Etienne would come all this way for me? He wouldn't even take a few days off to accompany me for Pops' funeral. I wouldn't take him back anyway, but every girl likes to feel like she's worth fighting for sometimes.

I return to my table and struggle to climb up onto the high-top bar stool to finish my drink. My mind starts to race, thinking of all the things I've discovered in the past few weeks. The noise around me starts to fade and people get...fuzzy. Maybe it's time for me to leave. I try to get my phone out of my pocket to call a cab, but it gets caught and as I tug firmly, breaking it free it sends the chair off balance. It teeters for a second and I try to reach for the edge of the table, but my reflexes are impaired, so I miss and hit the floor with a loud crashing thud. Jake and Ben push their way past people to get to me.

"Are you okay?" Jake asks, as he helps me to my feet.

"I'm fine," I assure him.

"You're done," Ben advises as he stands up the chair. "Give me your keys."

I flash him a look.

"Now!" he says sternly.

His bossiness makes me feel defensive. "Why are you always demanding my keys? I wasn't going to drive. I was going to call a cab," I argue.

"There are no cabs at this hour that are going to drive you all the way out there."

"I'll drive you," a voice adds from somewhere behind us.

We both turn to look at Gums, who has wandered over to check out the commotion.

"That's a HELL NO!" Ben answers for me.

He gives Ben the once-over, and decides he's not going to pick this battle. "One last dance then?"

Ben clenches his jaw. "Listen, buddy. She's not going anywhere with you, so go back to your bar stool and find someone else to bother."

Anger pumps adrenaline through my veins. "Now just a minute! You don't decide who drives me home, and who I can dance with. I'll dance with whomever I want."

"Cora." He gives me a warning look.

I stagger past him and grab Gums by the arm, a decision I regret the minute we hit the dance floor. Feeling a little cocky, he tries to flaunt his victory in front of Ben. He's busier than a randy octopus on aphrodisiacs, and my continual defensive moves are starting to wear me out. When he grabs my ass and tries to pull me in for a kiss, I muster all the strength I have to fight him off. Suddenly he's jerked away from me, as Ben grabs him by the scruff of the neck and tosses him a few feet to the side like a rag doll.

Ben and I stand face-to-face in the middle of the room. My heart pounds like a hammer in my chest. "Say goodnight to your friend."

I dare not argue, and to be honest, I don't have any fight left in me. I'm startled as Gums gets to his feet and flies at Ben in a testosterone-fueled rage. I scream trying to warn him as he's hit from behind. Everyone cringes as they watch Gums crash into Ben like a bug hitting a windshield, then slide down the mountain of muscle onto the floor. Ben gives his brother an agitated look and shakes his head in disbelief.

"It's time to go home," he says to me, as he takes two large strides toward me and lifts me over his shoulder.

"Ben!" I squeal as I'm hauled across the room. The amused look on Jake's face is the last thing I see as Ben shoves open the door and exits into the parking lot.

The rigid shoulder digging into my stomach starts to make me feel nauseous. "Would you put me down, please?" I request in a soft tone, trying not to agitate him any further. He ignores me until he gets to my car and then sets me down. I do my best not to sway, but I'm still feeling the effects of the alcohol.

"Get in the car, I'm driving you home. You don't get to make any more decisions for yourself tonight."

I'm not in any shape to argue with him, so I reach in my pocket for my keys. Boy, I must have had a lot to drink. He's already got them in his hand, and I don't even remember giving them to him. He opens the door and I try to get into the passenger seat, making it look like I'm completely sober. I might have pulled it off if I didn't get one leg stuck getting in and slide the rest of the way, whacking my head off the doorframe. "I'm okay," I assure him. Ben shakes his head and closes the door. Good Lord, now I'm tipsy *and* seeing stars.

Ben reaches over and grabs my seat belt and pulls it across me to buckle it in. I begin to giggle. I can't help it.

"Wait!" I yell as he puts it in reverse.

"What's the matter?" he asks startled.

"Are *you* okay to drive?"

"Yes."

"I dunno, I saw you drinking beer."

Ben rubs his eyes and sighs his frustration. "You saw me drink one beer."

"Okay, okay. You win."

The first few minutes of the drive I spend in quiet reflection. The past several weeks has been an emotional roller-coaster ride.

Ben glances over at me. "You're not going to be sick, are you?"

"No."

"Why are you so quiet? It makes me nervous."

"Good." I lean back in my seat, trying not to fall victim to the melancholy that's known to follow a good drunk.

Ben glances at me. "Let me ask you something, why did you end up at that bar tonight?"

I shrug. "I just wanted to get away from everything for a little while. It's been a shit day."

I stare at his dark silhouette, waiting for the moment when his rugged jawline is lightly illuminated by the street lights as we pass by. A heavy sadness starts to wash over me. "It's been a shit few weeks, actually."

"Where's lover boy? Why didn't he come back with you this time?"

"He and I aren't together anymore." I turn away to hide the tears that fill my eyes, and pretend I'm watching the moonlit scenery out the window.

Ben's jaw tenses. "He was cheating on you, wasn't he?"

I sniffle. "With his secretary. Who's now *my* secretary, since he got fired. That's the only reason I got this promotion."

He grumbles expletives under his breath. "You got the promotion because you work hard and you're good at what you do. *He* is a lowlife douchebag who doesn't deserve you," Ben says in a soft tone, interrupting my downhearted silence.

I sniffle. "I'm not exactly an angel."

"True. But that's no excuse for what he did to you. There's no excuse for cheating. He's not a good man."

Tears stream down my face and I don't even care about hiding my sorrow anymore. As we pull up in front of my home, I look for my nana in the kitchen window like I do every time I pull in. The new motion light makes me squint as we stop in front of it and it glares obnoxiously bright, as if we've just driven into the middle of an alien abduction.

"I'll adjust that tomorrow," he promises.

Tomorrow is Sunday. Doesn't he ever rest? I don't move to get out of the car. A heaviness has pinned me to my seat, as I grieve over the recent discovery about my mother's death and feel apprehensive about going into the house.

He opens the door and extends his hand to help me out. Still a little impaired, I fall into him. He's wearing the same cologne as he was at my pops' funeral, and I linger too long against his chest. It's hard to pull myself away, but I do, and then take a slow, careful stroll toward the house with him following protectively. Once inside, I stand quietly in the dark hallway, hesitating before running my hand along the wall and flipping on the light switch.

"Why does it always feel so cold in here?" I wonder aloud.

"Don't complain, the farmer's almanac says we're in for one of the hottest, driest summers and it'll be here soon. I could start the fire, if you want."

He doesn't wait for an answer. I watch as he builds a fire with the few remaining pieces of kindling left in the house.

I feel like I should be doing something. "Would you like a coffee, a tea, or a sandwich?"

"No, I'm fine." He closes the screen and turns to face me. "I should get going." He drops my keys on the table.

I glance up the dark stairwell to the second floor and get a shiver. "Ben, wait!"

He looks at me startled. "What's wrong?"

"Please stay."

I sense his apprehension and scramble for words, unsure how to verbalize how I'm feeling. "I don't want to be here alone right now," I implore. "You can stay in the spare bedroom."

I turn slowly and look up into his meadow green eyes. So much is said within that moment of intense silence between us.

"All right, I'll stay.

I let out an audible sigh of relief. "Thank you." I lead him upstairs and down the hallway, trying hard not to sway.

"That is my mother's room," I slur as I point to the closed door. "It's exactly the way she left it when she died."

"We won't disturb anything in there, tonight," Ben promises.

I continue down the hall and stand at the door to my grandparents' room and hesitate. "Are you sure you're okay with me staying in here?"

"Yes. Of course." I stare at his lips. His mouth looks warm and inviting. "Cora?"

"Hmmm?" I ask dreamily.

"Do you need help getting ready for bed?"

"No. I'm fine!" I insist as I sway forward, bringing my lips within a tempting distance. I can feel the warmth of his breath and close my eyes.

"Well, good night," he says, turning the doorknob and taking a step away from me.

"Good night." I retire to my own room. I turn on the bedside lamp and try to get undressed, but I keep tipping over, so I lean against the wall while I change into a pair of sleep shorts and a T-shirt. When I turn to face the room, the old travel trunk is in the middle of the floor. I jump, startled at its appearance there. I push it back in front of the closet door, where I'm sure that I left it earlier, and get into bed. I sit for a moment, feeling unnerved, when something catches my eye. A monarch butterfly sits on the windowsill, gently fluttering its wings. "What the...?"

I stub my toe on the bedpost and curse as I gently swoosh it out the open window and pull the pane down tight. Shadows bloom and disappear around the room and I blink my eyes, trying to convince myself I'm seeing things that aren't really there. I remind myself to never drink again, as I scan the room with a heightened awareness. Suddenly, a chill fills the room, making me shiver. I jump into bed and pull the covers over my head, but the multitude of blankets do nothing to warm me. I toss them aside and get to my feet. I'd run if I could, but I'm still a little wobbly so I run my fingertips along the wall to help guide me down the hall.

I knock once, lightly, then push open the door.

Ben opens his eyes. "What's wrong?"

Can I tell him there's monsters in my room? Probably not. I stand at the side of his bed, like a small child looking for comfort. "I'm cold. Can I sleep with you?"

He lifts the edge of the blanket and welcomes me in without saying a word. I don't hesitate to crawl in beside him.

He pulls the blankets over me, ensuring the I'm completely covered. I tuck in under his arm, pressing as close as I can, seeking more warmth.

"Thank you," I whisper, trying not to think about how good it feels to have his body so close to me. Ben tenses, and I wonder if he's fighting the same thoughts. Suddenly the room begins to spin. 'Whoa!"

"Put one foot on the floor," Ben says in a gruff, sleepy voice.

"What?" I ask confused.

"Put one foot on the floor. It'll stop the bed from spinning."

I position myself onto my back and lift the blanket, letting my foot slide heavily down the side of the bed and rest on the floor. "Hey! It works," I exclaim surprised.

"Mmhmm."

"How'd you know?"

He moves, trying to put some space between us. "It's not my first rodeo. There's been a night or two I've had a few too many." He ends his sentence with a loud snore.

I look around the room, not sure what I'm looking for, but hoping I find nothing. When the room finally stops spinning, I roll over toward the middle of the bed and attempt to hijack Ben's body heat. With his guard down, he turns on his side and puts his arm over me, pulling me close and securing me to him. I get a strange feeling of déjà vu, or maybe it's desire, but whatever it is, this moment feels...right. I open one eye and survey the room to make sure everything is still in its place before I drift off to sleep in his arms.

CHAPTER TWELVE

The next morning, I wake up alone. It's a toss-up between feeling relieved and being disappointed. Feeling a little dehydrated, I get up. The minute I open the bedroom door, I smell the delicious aromatic fragrance of coffee and bacon.

I glance around when I get to the bottom of the stairs, but he's not here so I wander into the kitchen. I grab a piece of bacon off the plate, take a bite, and read the note strategically placed by the coffee maker.

It reads... *In case you're wondering, this time you did drool. Jake brought me a dry shirt and we've gone in to town to buy supplies. You need to drink juice this morning to help with rehydration. I figure you'll ignore me and drink the coffee anyway, so I left acetaminophen tablets beside the mugs.*

I catch myself smiling as I open the lid, dump two pills in my hand, and wash them down with a mouthful of black coffee.

I refill my mug and grab a stack of paperwork I took out of the file cabinet in the office. The back deck looks inviting and I would probably benefit from the fresh air. When I step through the sliding glass patio doors, the sun blinds me. I curse and squint, hoping that the acetaminophen kicks in quickly.

I organize the folders by date and spread them out across the patio table, systematically going through them from oldest to newest. I'm amazed at the documents Nana kept for all these years and intrigued as to why she thought she'd need them. I take the last sip of coffee and sit back in the chair, perplexed. They kept a folder full of forty-year-old receipts for every chicken they purchased at the livestock exchange, but not my birth certificate?

A sudden loud bang makes me jump. I can tell by the loud pounding that follows; the boys are back. I shelter my eyes from the sun and follow the wraparound deck to the front of the house. I'm relieved to see I finally have a new window where the hole used to be. I watch as they meticulously match the siding and replace the trim.

Ben looks up and notices me standing there. "When we're finished, you won't be able to tell what's new and what's been here for eighty years."

"How's your head?" Jake asks with a smirk.

"A little fuzzy, but I'm all right." I ignore the snickering from a few of the guys who were with them last night.

"Knock it off," Ben warns.

I must still be drunk because I think he just smiled and winked at me.

I hear an approaching vehicle and turn to watch the shiny new SUV of my real estate lady come up the dirt drive and stop in front of the house.

"I wonder what she wants?" I say aloud.

Ben wipes the sweat from his brow with the bottom of his T-shirt. I can't help but stare at the well-defined, chiseled abs.

"She's probably just checking on your progress."

I nod, trying not to think about how I was pressed against his body all night. "You're probably right."

"Hi there!" she yells as she gets out of the SUV. Her loud cheerful voice is like a sharp rusty nail, driven directly into my forehead. "Hey! It's starting to look great!"

"Thank you," I say in a softer tone.

"How are things going inside? Have you got rid of that clutter?"

"Not yet. I've only been back a few days, but I'm working on it."

"Great. It's such a beautiful day, it would be a good day to get working on the landscaping."

"Landscaping?" I ask confused. "It's a farm."

"Well, yes. But it will make it easier to sell if we tidied it up a little. At least if we just look after an acre or two directly around the house."

Ben stops what he's doing and pays attention.

"Okay," I look around at the muddy walkways and bare gardens. "I'm not sure where to start."

"Start with cutting that long grass between the house and the barn. People are going to want to know what the land looks like."

"*I* don't even remember what the land looks like."

"It wouldn't hurt to get a fresh coat of paint on the barn, either."

Ben raises his eyebrows when I nod my head in agreement. The truth is, today I just don't have the energy to object. I walk with her around the property and take several more notes before walking her back to her SUV.

I wave as she leaves, and then stand in the driveway with the palms of my hands on my temples.

I can feel Ben watching me as I walk out to the old shed. Dust flies through the air as I whip open the door and the breeze flows inside, for the first time in many years, I'm sure. I struggle, as I pull out an old lawnmower that's tangled up in a brittle piece of garden hose. Let's see if I can remember how to get this thing started. I pull the cord, only to have it jerk my arm and stop a foot out. Slowly I let the cord reel back in and give it another hard yank. I look down at the gas cap and I'm amazed at just how stupid I can be sometimes. I've been away for far too long.

When I come out of the shed with an old metal gasoline can, I notice everybody watching me. I pretend I'm not aware of them and fill the tank to the top, then screw on the cap. "Here goes nothing." My first attempt has the cord creep out slowly and stop. I guess I need a little more muscle. I put my foot on the top of the mower and pull with everything I've got. A huge feeling of accomplishment washes over me when it starts. I glance over at Ben, but he's climbed up on the roof and is fixing the eavestrough. As I push the heavy mower toward the long grass it starts to putter, and then stalls. I try several times to get it started again, but I think this time it's done.

"The gas was probably too old," Ben yells from the roof.

Cursing I push it over to an accumulating pile of junk I need to get rid of. A rusty old push mower catches my eye. I move it back and forth on the short grass and watch clippings spray through the air. When I get to the longer grass, I push until the muscles in my arms start to shake. It becomes heavier the farther I get into the denser grass, so I lean the handle against my chest to help get some weight behind it as I push. The grass bends beneath the blades, but it doesn't cut. I stop and exhale a frustrated breath. This is too much work. I try to walk backward but the long meadow grass tangles around the rusty edges like a vine and holds me there. I glance over at Ben and catch him watching me as he climbs down off the ladder.

I give the handle a strong tug, freeing it from the tangled vegetation with such force that I fly backward, lose my footing, and land on my ass. I hear a few muffled chuckles from the direction of the house. I look at the broken handle still clutched in my hand and I hear Pops' words. "Never give up, even if you break a lot of eggs until you get it right." I pick up the broken pieces of the push mower and toss them, too, into the junk pile. If nothing else, I should make a killing on selling scrap metal.

I slide the doors of the old barn open, one at a time, letting light into the space and I grab the old baseball cap that hangs on a hook by the key rack. It takes me a few minutes of fiddling with the three-point hitch, but when I drive that old tractor through the doors and into the sunlight hauling the bush hog, everyone stops what they're doing and stares. I smile. Ben is right. Once a country girl, always a country girl. It's in my blood.

Speaking of Ben, why is he running toward me, waving his arms and yelling?

"Cora! Hang on a minute."

"What?" I yell, over the loud rumbling of the tractor engine.

"Wait a minute," he yells again as he grabs the steering wheel and pulls himself up onto the deck beside me. I slow to a stop and wait for him to catch his breath.

"What are you doing?"

I squint. "I'm going to cut the grass like Fiona said."

"You can't just go rolling through long grass like that with the bush hog."

"I can't?"

"Noooo."

"Why can't I? That's what bush hogs are for."

He reaches over and shuts off the key. "You've been away too long."

"What does that have to do with anything? I can still drive a tractor."

"Your grandfather was a farmer."

I furrow my brow. "Thanks, Captain Obvious. Do you have a point to make? My head is pounding, and I'd like to get this done."

A muscle in his jaw twitches. "I bet you got a lot of spankings as a child,"

"Maybe," I say taunting him.

"You need one, right now." he says in frustration.

My face turns a shade of scarlet and the moment becomes awkward as he studies my reaction and waits for a response. I'm speechless. I can't control the surge of hormones that makes my lady parts twitch. He gives his head a slight shake, as if he's trying to free himself of the image in his mind. "Farmers don't ever take anything to the dump, Cora. They just discard it somewhere out on the property or use it to fill in holes in the land. You have no idea what's out there, hidden in the tall grass."

His eyes narrow with concern. "If you hit something with this thing, or drop into a hidden hole, you could hurt yourself."

I survey the property, curious about what could be out there. "What do you suggest then?"

"Walk the property first."

A line appears between my brows.

"I'll help you."

"Don't you have work to do?" I glance over at the house.

He brushes my shoulder as he puts his hand on the back of the tractor seat. "Jake can handle it. Once we know the land is clear you can let loose with your bush hog."

I smirk. "That sounds kind of dirty."

He ignores me and hops down off the tractor before lifting me to the ground. His hands linger on my waist a few minutes longer than needed once I've found my footing.

"Where do we start?"

"North to south, up and down. Then east to west until we've covered it all."

"That will take all day."

"It'll go faster than you think. Are you afraid of spiders?"

"No."

"Good, there are some big ones out there. Grab one of those big branches and break off all the little twigs."

My eyes open wide. "Are they ninja spiders? We need weapons?"

"No, you need a walking stick to feel out the ground in front of you. You don't want to twist an ankle in a weasel hole."

"That's true, I don't." I start to walk toward the edge of the long grass.

"And it helps to scare away the snakes," he adds.

I stop dead in my tracks. "I'm going to pretend I didn't hear that." I'm only a few feet in when I hit my first obstacle. "What do I do with stuff we find?" I ask, holding up an old milk crate.

"Start a pile, and we'll get Caleb to load it onto the trailer later and haul it up."

I'm shocked at how quickly the pile grows. Ben wasn't kidding. There are years and years of discarded household items and busted farm equipment hidden in the long grass. "What's this?" I ask, holding up a small cylindrical object.

"Shotgun shell."

"There's a lot of them right here."

"Probably warning shots for the coyotes."

"Or the Indians," I laugh as I hold up a broken arrow.

Ben simpers, "I doubt the natives used plastic tip arrows."

"Fair point." I hold it up and examine it more closely, before walking over and discarding it on the pile of junk. On top of the growing mound of broken flowerpots and shingles, something catches my eye. I pick up a mud-crusted figurine and begin to brush off some of the dirt. "Hello, there. Where did you come from?"

"Who are you talking to?" Ben asks, curiously.

I turn to show him the faded garden gnome.

"I found him in a hole over here."

"I remember this guy. He used to sit in the garden by the front porch."

"I've never seen one sitting down and leaning back like that. I've only seen ones standing up."

"My pops once told me there was an old story his grandfather used to tell him about gnomes who protected the farm. If anybody should see them, they would freeze on the spot."

"Is that what you think happened to that guy?"

"You never know."

"He's seen better days, that's for sure."

I go back to following my path through the meadow with my stick in one hand and the gnome tucked under my arm.

"Errrr, what are you doing?"

"I can't leave him all alone over there."

"It's junk now. All the paints worn off," Ben reasons.

Shocked, my head snaps to the side to look at him. "What are you suggesting, Mr. Restoration Expert? I should just throw him away becomes he's old and worn?"

"You're funny," he says, walking parallel to me a few feet away. "Shit!" he wails, as something large and hard connects with his shins.

Alarmed by his continued cursing, I make way toward him. "Are you okay?"

"Yes," he says agitated, as he rubs his shin.

"What did you hit?"

Ben pulls at the long grass, ripping it away from a large wooden object. "What is that? Part of an old barn?"

I know what this is. "It's the original front door." A strange shiver runs through me. "Is it still in one piece?"

Ben walks around the edges, tearing away weeds and grass that has grown over it. Securing his hands delicately under the edge, he tries to lift it. It budges a few inches before he looks up at me and gently places it back on the ground. "It's rotten."

"I know, I recognized the noise. It's the same sound the deck made as it disintegrated beneath me."

"Hey, what's this pile over here?" he asks moving to a stacked of discarded wood. "It looks like hand-cut scroll work." He lifts one of the pieces in the air. "Was this trim on the house somewhere?"

I kneel on the ground beside the door and reach out to touch the wood. Placing my hand on it transports me back in time.

"Cora? What's wrong?"

I get to my feet, my eyes flooded with tears. "I wasn't very old, but I remember the day my mother painted this door. *Tangerine Orange*, she said it was called."

"It's an unusual colour for a door in those days."

"My mother was an artist. She loved colour. I liked it because it reminded me of the monarch butterflies that were always in the front garden."

"Why are you upset?" Ben asks moving to my side.

"For years, my grandmother told me my mother picked this colour because it was welcoming and happy, and that it would make anyone smile when they got here. She said it would let people know they'd find love and hope inside our home." I pause, trying to sort out my thoughts. Ben brushes his hand up and down my arm, trying to console me. "I don't understand, Ben. Why the *illusion* of happiness?"

"Why do you think it was an illusion? Your grandparents seemed loving."

"If my mother was happy, why did she kill herself?"

"I don't know the answer to that Cora."

"When I was a teenager, I overheard my pops talking to someone about that old door. I heard him say that they were short of cash and the only paint available was half a gallon of orange paint they found in the barn. They used to use it to mark the date on crates of produce they took to market."

Ben's expression dulls.

"It feels like there are so many lies around my childhood memories," I sniffle. "I thought my mother loved me. I thought I made her happy. To find out that she made a choice to take her own life and leave me here alone..."

Ben pulls me into his chest. "Don't. Don't drive yourself crazy thinking things like that. Thirty years ago, there wasn't awareness around mental health like today. She must have been in a very dark place to feel like that was her only way out."

I rest my head on his shoulder. Ben draws in a long breath and caresses my back. In this moment, there's a shift in our relationship and for the first time I admit to myself what these feelings really are. "It's from the porch roof," I finally say, changing the subject and trying to nudge away the feelings.

"Excuse me?"

"The scrolled, wooden trim used to be on the edge of the roof that covered the porch. It collapsed under the weight of the snow several winters ago. Pop never bothered to rebuild it."

"I'd love to see what it looked like. Do you have any pictures of the house before she started falling apart?"

"Somewhere in all the boxes of stuff in there. I'll look for you."

A gentle breeze blows a smoky cloud toward us and the smell of burning wood.

"We should probably go see what's going on," I say, pulling myself out of his arms.

"The guys must have lit a fire to burn the scrap."

"I'm not lucky enough for the house to burn down." I reach down and pick up my gnome like it's a priceless treasure.

Ben gives me a sympathetic smile and reaches out his hand and I take it as I step out of the long grass. His expression turns to sadness. "Nothing that happened in the past, is your fault. You do know that, right?"

I nod and release his hand as we start to walk up the hill toward the house. The afternoon sun is low in the sky, and it ignites the horizon with a magnificent bright orange glow as it sets behind the trees. Tangerine orange to be exact. Ben notices it too and gently brushes his fingers against mine as we walk. It's at that moment I feel a glimmer of the happiness Nana once told me she felt here. This doesn't feel like a lie.

Jeff and Caleb are getting ready to head home. Ben thanks them and walks them to their truck. The fire is almost burned out when he returns, and he helps me move my chair closer to the firepit to keep out of the chilly evening air. Unfolding a jacket, he's taken out of the truck, he drapes it over my shoulders, and untucks my hair from beneath the collar. Jake watches, curious about our behaviour as he rakes the coals to make sure there are no flare-ups.

"Are you ready to go home, brother?" he asks.

"Actually, why don't you go on ahead, Jake? I was hoping to get a photo of the house that shows the original front porch. Cora is going to look for one for me." He turns to me for my approval. The flames of the fire reflect in his eyes and I'm momentarily mesmerized. "Is that okay, Cora?" he prompts.

"Of course. You're probably starving. I can make dinner."

"I would never say no to food."

We chuckle. Jake looks between us as he dumps a pail of water over the last of the red-hot embers. "I think I like it better when you two are butting heads." He digs his keys out of his pocket and walks to the truck. "This is just weird."

CHAPTER THIRTEEN

Ben follows me into the house.

"I've put all the photo albums I've found so far together in one spot." The breeze has picked up and blows the curtains away from the open windows. Suddenly I panic. "Oh no!"

"What?" Ben asks, as I rush to the patio door.

"I left everything outside on the table." I gather it up quickly and take a quick look around for anything that blew away. "That was a close one," I admit as I drop everything in a pile on the coffee table.

"What's all that?" Ben ask curiously.

"Paperwork out of my grandparents' filing cabinet. I've been looking for my birth certificate."

"Oh?"

"Yeah, I was hoping my mother listed my father on it. He hasn't bothered looking for me in the thirty years, but I'd still like to know who he is."

"Can't you send away for a copy of it?"

"I filled out the request online and it didn't give me any results."

"That seems odd."

"I know, right? It said there was an error in my search, and I should call the office during business hours. I'll do that this week." I walk toward the kitchen. "I have leftover pizza, are you hungry?"

"Yeah, don't bother heating it up, I like it cold."

I return with the greasy cardboard box and a couple of beers. "Me too. It seems like the only time I order pizza is when I'm really busy, and then it sits on the counter until I remember to eat."

I raise my brow as I watch him fold a piece in half and practically inhale it. "Hey, look at this." I reach for the folder on the top of the pile. "I found the sales receipt for that old farm truck."

Ben takes it out of my hand and looks it over. "I love that old truck. This is really cool. Look how much they paid for it back then," he laughs.

"There are stacks and stacks of old receipts and manuals. I think every cancelled cheque they ever wrote is in that box over there."

"Crazy, the things they hold on to. I remember sorting through some of the paperwork my mother kept all those years." He scratches his head and looks down at the paperwork pensively. "You said they didn't get rid of anything in your mothers' room, right?"

"Right."

"Did your mother have a desk or file cabinet?"

"Yes."

"Would your nana have your birth certificate? Or would it be in with your mom's stuff?"

I tilt my head to the side. "I guess I should have started there."

"Maybe. It's just a thought."

Ben follows as I head up the narrow stairs to the second floor. I always get a nervous feeling when I open this door and enter her room. When I was younger, I used to sneak in here when Nana was out shopping. I would sit for hours and read a book, or just watch the chickens peck around the yard from the window. Sometimes when I was in there, I would get a heavy oppressive feeling that weighed on me for days. I have that feeling now.

"Are you okay?" Ben asks concerned.

"Sure," I lie. "Aunt Bea says my grandmother had a knack for hiding things and she wouldn't be surprised if my mother did too." We open every drawer and search for hidden compartments in or beneath them. After searching every nook and cranny thoroughly, I sit on the side of the bed and frown.

"Either she didn't keep it, or my nana went through everything and took out what was important. It'll turn up eventually, even if have to get a copy from the government."

"Hey, is this you?" Ben holds up a baby picture.

"I think so."

He turns it over and shrugs. "It says Maggie on the back of it."

"That's odd." I take it out of his hand and study it. "I'm positive this is me." I get to my feet. "I'll put it with the rest of the photos in my room."

I hurry down the hallway and grab the album from the top of the pile. "I love old black and white photos." I smile as I flip through the first few pages, stopping to examine more carefully a picture of a very young Aunt Beatrice and a dashing young man. I look up to find Ben standing in the doorway, staring at with me with an ardor I've never seen in his eyes. "Are you going to come in?" I ask in a demure tone.

He gives me a coy smile. "Do you think your pops would approve of you having a boy in your room?"

"Well that would depend on your intentions, Mr. McCarthy," I say in jest, batting my eyelashes. The energy in the room heightens as he takes a step toward me, and his gaze locks to mine. The temperature in the room rockets to a hundred degrees, despite the cool breeze that's gently blowing the curtains on the other side of the room.

"I intend to kiss you," he says in a deep masculine tone, as he closes the space between us. I feel his chest expand as he fills his lungs with air before he presses his lips against mine in a tender kiss. My eyes flutter open, as the warmth of his mouth fades away. I think about turning him away but *want* pulses through me, prompting me to rake my fingers through his hair and pull him closer, encouraging him to lean in and claim my lips again. Anticipation heightens my arousal, and he doesn't disappoint me. Parting his lips, he deepens his kiss until his exchange of breath becomes intoxicating.

He yanks his shirt off over his head and drops it. The view of his muscular chest and tatted arms, revs up my desire.

"Do you have any idea what it did to me waking up beside you this morning?" he asks in a rough, low tone.

Unable to voice any reasonable thoughts, I shake my head.

"I've been craving you all day."

My knees bend under his gentle command, sitting me down on the edge of the bed. His arousal strains against the fabric of his jeans. Thick and pulsing, he continues to harden as I undo the zipper and yank them to the floor.

When he joins me on the bed, my body burns beneath his touch. As he explores every curve, he strips me of my clothing and discards it. I exhale a needy moan as his hands skim over the swell of my bottom and then grip deeply into the soft flesh, pulling me firmly against his body.

He teases my nipple with his warm, wet tongue and when the cool air of the room hardens it more, he nips it between his teeth. When I cry out, his body tenses like it's almost his undoing. He raises his head and takes a deliberate slow breath to regain his control.

Staring into his eyes, I run my hands down his muscular chest to his waist, brushing gently across the tip of his hard cock. His nostrils flare, and he lowers his mouth to mine, owning me with a possessive kiss as he moves his body over mine, supporting himself on strong biceps.

Spreading my legs wider, I invite him in and gasp with his first thrust. He growls and settles into a slow languid rhythm that has my body climbing to the breaking point. I circle my hips and push against him, trying to sate the ache. Ben responds with deliberate strokes, the friction pushing me over the edge into explosive waves of pleasure. He growls a harsh curse and slams into me hard, simultaneously meeting his release.

Once he finds presence of mind, he eases off me and lies by my side. Without any delay, he pulls me closer to him and presses a kiss on my forehead. His skin is damp and radiating warmth but being this close to him feels amazing.

I let out a small giggle and he tilts his head to look at me. "What?"

"Nothing."

"Oh no, you don't get to play that game. What's so funny?"

"I didn't peg you for a *post-coital cuddler*."

"No?" he says, pretending to be wounded.

"No," I laugh.

"I don't know why you'd say that. I'm a very cuddly guy."

"Compared to a rattlesnake, maybe."

"That's harsh. I have to say, I never thought I'd hear the words *coital* and *cuddler* ever used together in the same sentence."

I laugh a moment. Ben brushes my hair away from my face. "I love that sound."

"Of me snorting?"

"Of you, being happy. And sexually satisfied."

I raise a brow. "Well, that's kind of presumptuous."

"Oh, I'm not presuming anything. I know for a fact."

"Oh, you do, do you?"

"Mmhmm. I was there. I felt it."

"Maybe I was faking it."

He laughs once. "You were definitely NOT faking it."

"No, I wasn't," I admit. My eyes sparkle and he tilts his head to the side.

"Well," he says, pulling me closer and kissing my lips. "I better make sure."

I protest, as the warmth of his mouth surrounds a sensitive nipple. "What are you doing?"

He stops and raises his eyes. "I'm going to make sure you're so sexually satisfied that you're walking funny tomorrow."

"I've got a lot to do tomorrow." I say, struggling for control and failing. "I need to have feeling in the lower half of my body."

"I don't really care." He grins, then holds me down with gentle pressure until I surrender to his warm roaming tongue.

Suddenly, the window pane slams shut so hard that things on the desk vibrate and go crashing to the floor.

"What the hell?" Ben says startled, lifting his head.

"There's been some weird things going on in this house since I got home."

He looks at me concerned. "You don't think I upset your pops, do you?"

"If you did, he just left." I put my hand on the top of his head and direct him downward. "Carry on."

CHAPTER FOURTEEN

"Good morning," Ben says in a cheerful voice, as he reaches the bottom of the stairs.

"Good morning. I made you eggs, just the way you like them."

"And coffee?"

"Yes, I hope it's not too strong. I'm used to the kind where you pop the premeasured pods into the top."

"It can't be any worse than Jake's."

"I also found this." I hand him a photo that I found of my Nana in the garden which shows the entire front porch of the house. He grins as he studies.

"What are you working on?" he asks, looking at my laptop.

"Sorry, work emails." I look over the top of the screen as he walks into the kitchen and do a double take when I notice he's wearing nothing but his jeans. He returns with a coffee cup in his hand and sits down on the couch.

"How's that project going?"

"It's going well." I lower the screen, so I can see him. It's nice to have someone interested in conversation in the morning, and if I'm being honest, I didn't peg him as a morning person. "I think I've come up with an angle."

"An angle?"

"Yeah, that's the business. Everybody has an angle or a goal. Every target market has a weakness. Every minute of every day someone is out there spinning the truth and enhancing the details, trying to find the angle that will manipulate the masses into thinking they need their products or use their resources. The endgame is to convert interest into cash."

Ben raises his eyebrows in a quick flash of understanding. "I never thought of it that way. Kind of feels sneaky and dishonest."

"Dishonest, no. Sneaky, perhaps. Sometimes people are highly susceptible to suggestion. Sometimes you have a really good product, but people don't know that they need it. Sometimes you have a good product or great service, and nobody knows you exist."

"Got ya."

"Let me ask you something, other than the trade shows you attend, how do you let people know about your business?"

"Word of mouth mostly."

"You don't have a website or Facebook page? Do you ever use social media to advertise?"

"Jake set up a website last year, but to be honest we don't put anything on it."

I'm not surprised. "Do you want to see the marketing ads we've created for this project? The artistic team has done a fantastic job at putting together the visuals for it?"

"Sure."

He moves beside me, and I flip through the commercial and advertisement graphics. I can feel his warm breath as he leans in toward me to watch the screen.

"These are awesome. You did these?"

"The ideas are mine, and the ads are based on what I envisioned the feel of the campaign to be. I'm not a graphic designer, so the art department puts them together with my instructions. Like... put a round thingy over here, and children playing and make them purple."

"Purple?"

I get embarrassed. "Not the children. Obviously, there are no purple children," I say flustered. "I'm just making a point."

He tucks a strand of hair behind my ear and smiles. "I'm just messing with you. I think this is amazing work."

My heart tingles. My grandparents were always supportive of me in everything I did, but this is something new for me. I've never been in a relationship with a man who was interested in my career and impressed with the work I do. Did I just think about this becoming a relationship? I blink my eyes, trying to remember what I was going to say. "Thank you. It was a lot easier to work from here than I thought. Less interruptions."

Ben tilts his head to the side. "Are you going to work from here, from now on then?"

My answer puts me in a somber mood. "Only temporarily. I have to be back in Paris to pitch my campaign to the clients in two weeks. I'm hoping to get things settled and the house on the market by then."

He goes silent and his expression hardens. I look down, feeling like I've just ruined something good. I stare at the tribal ink on his forearms and become curious. "Do your tattoos have any special meaning for you?"

He holds them out in front of us, turning his wrists so I can see all sides. He looks like he wants to say something but changes his mind. "No. I just liked them."

"Well, I suppose that's a good reason."

He rubs the back of his neck, still looking like there's something on his mind. I wait, but he says nothing as he puts his feet up on the coffee table and stretches out, getting comfortable. I go back to my emails, then sneak another look at his bare chest and broad shoulders. He adjusts his position, and I glance downward to notice that his pants are undone, and I have an interesting view. "Are you wearing underwear?" I ask amused.

"No."

I raise a brow. "Aren't you afraid, you know...*things* are going to get caught in your zipper?"

He lowers his brow, and nods. "Yes, that's why I left it undone."

"Are you going to sit there like that all morning?"

He grins. "Maybe, is it distracting you?"

"Kind of, yes."

"Good."

"No, not good. I have to get some work done."

"Do you want me to leave?"

"Yes. You and your muscly chest and your strong arms..." I wave my hands at the lower half of his body, "and all the other parts of you, need to go...away...now."

"All right. I have something I want to do this morning, so I'll go home for a while." He disappears upstairs to get his socks and shirt and I go back to concentrating on my emails.

He startles me as he leans over the laptop. "Jesus, woman, why are you so jumpy? I'm just going to give you a kiss."

"Sorry." I laugh as I lower the laptop screen. Ben lays a kiss on my lips and then skims across my cheek. His whiskers lightly chafe across my skin, and my thighs twitch as I have all sorts of inappropriate thoughts. "Go," I demand, pointing at the door.

Ben chuckles. "I'll be back in a few hours."

With my head down, staring at the computer screen, I wave as the screen door snaps shut with a bang. "Bye, see you later. Drive safe. Blah blah blah."

I rake my fingers through my hair, relieved that he's gone. Before I'm going to get anything accomplished, I think I need to take a cold shower and get dressed.

I got a lot accomplished this morning without any distractions. I watch Ben get out of the truck with his hair combed and beard neatly trimmed. I open the front door and stand out on the porch intrigued, as I watch him get something, seemingly fragile out of the back. I become even more enamored with him as he walks toward me and his smile curls at the corner of his mouth, softening the normally hard line of his jaw.

"What are you up to?"

"Just bringing home an old friend." He carefully unwraps the paper from around it.

"My gnome!" I squeal as I practically jump down the steps and race to him. "Ben!" I exclaim. "It's like brand-new!"

"I couldn't match the paint exactly, and I had to guess what colour to make his eyes."

"Oh, I didn't even think of that." I study them and smile. "You made them brown."

"I did. With little flecks of gold, just like yours."

I throw my arms around him.

"Careful! I didn't spend all that time fixing him up, to drop him, and have him smash into pieces."

"Put him down!"

"Where?"

I look around at the vacant flower bed in front of the nonexistent porch. "Anywhere, I guess."

Ben carefully places him in the garden and stands back to admire his work.

"I'm going to call him Gordon," I announce.

"Why Gordon?"

"Because he kind of looks like my lawyer."

Ben laughs.

"Except he looks a lot happier than my lawyer."

"Your lawyer will probably look happier when you settle up his bill."

I wrinkle my nose. "Probably very true." I look at Ben, and I notice there's a lot more going on than just the coiffed hair; he's wearing nice clothes and cologne.

I don't trust his mischievous grin. "What's going on?"

"When was the last time you've been downtown Orangeville?

I shrug. "It's been years, why?"

"I'm meeting a client for lunch, and I'd like you to join me."

"Oh, well I don't want to intrude, or get in the way."

"You won't. I want you there. Go put on one of those pretty designer outfits from France."

"To go downtown Orangeville?"

"Yup. It's changed since you left. Trust me, you won't be overdressed."

I like the thought of getting dressed in my own clothes and going out. I do miss spending time in Paris' entertainment district.

"You've got ten minutes to get ready."

I run into the house and get ready in seven minutes, and gloat about it all the way into town.

Ben rolls his eyes and ignores me. "We've got some time before lunch. I thought we'd take a drive through town."

My head darts from left to right taking everything in. "Look at the tree carvings!" I say excitedly.

"There's a whole bunch of them now. You can do a walking tour to see them."

"Wow, look at all the new shops and restaurants. Some of these buildings look brand-new."

Ben beams with pride.

"Did you do the restorations on them?"

"Some of them."

"I think I can tell which ones you worked on. You have a very distinctive style to your work, even though it's restorative."

"The annoying perfectionist style?" He smirks.

"You did a great job," I affirm. "I love how you made them beautiful again, instead of tearing them down and being bullied into modernization.

"Some we just couldn't save structurally, so they required architects and people experienced in demolition. I do think they honoured our history and matched the surrounding architecture to the feel of the town."

He parks at a lot at the end of town and we get out and walk. I stop and look through the window of an art gallery that consigns all types of work from local artists. There's a specific stained-glass object dangling in the window display that catches my eye as it sparkles and refracts the sunlight.

"We can go in and look around, if you want." Ben holds open the door and I walk down the aisles feeling like I've just made an incredible discovery. I've never seen so many beautiful things together in one spot, except for some of the museums in France. Ben disappears around the corner, and I continue to take in all the paintings and sculptures for sale.

When he reappears around the other side of the display, he has a small paper bag in his hand. "Ready? I'm getting hungry."

"Where are we eating?" I ask, as we step out onto the street and into the warm sunlight.

"My favourite little café, not too far down."

Ben moves closer to me, to allow an elderly woman with a walker more room. I enjoy the possessive gesture as his hand brushes mine, and he intertwines our fingers. Ben yells at a driver for jumping forward impatiently as we ignore the red flashing crosswalk sign and rush across the street.

I glance up at the architecture of the old building that looks like it's been here since the beginning of time. Heavy wooden beams and patterned brick masonry add to its charm. Ben grins as he opens the door and ushers me to a table by the window. "I must say, this is nothing like I expected. There must be a lot of local history here."

"It's one of my favourite places. It's changed hands a few times and undergone some major restorations over the years."

"It's gorgeous," I admit.

Ben opens a menu and passes it across the table to me. "They call it a café, but the food here is some of the best fine dining I've had."

"Well that's impressive, considering I know how much you love to eat."

Ben tips his head in acknowledgement. By the time the waitress brings us our drinks, the place is packed and there's a wait time for a table. The quiet, intimate setting is now humming with pleasant chatter.

"What time will your client be here?"

"She's already here."

I turn to look behind me and see a woman approaching, but she stops and takes a seat at another table.

I look at Ben confused, and he smiles.

"Where?"

"Sitting right here, across from me."

"I'm your client?"

"I'm doing some work for you, aren't I?"

"Well, yes. You're helping me with a few things, but..." Ben waits for me to finish my thought and I realize there's no point in it. "What's in the bag?"

"A bribe." He pushes the small paper bag across the table.

I pick it up, feeling suspicious as I carefully unroll the top and slide out the contents. I'm dumbfounded, and I look up at Ben with a stunned look. "It's beautiful." I hold up the stained-glass monarch butterfly, so it catches the sun through the café window.

"I noticed you admiring it. I wanted to put a smile on your face today."

"Don't I smile?"

"You're starting to. I get that you've had a lot to deal with lately."

"Thank you." I carefully wrap it back up in the paper bag and put it to the side when the waitress brings our food. I'm only a few bites in, when I notice a look of terror warp across his face. A woman stops at my side and there's an uncomfortable silent exchange between the two of them before she speaks.

"Hello, Ben."

"Hello, Meghan."

"It's been a long time. You're looking well."

Ben fidgets uncomfortably. "Thanks."

"Hi, I'm Cora," I extend my hand, hoping to break the tension.

"Nice to meet you. I'll let you two alone to finish your lunch. I just wanted to say hello."

"You should have just kept on walking," Ben says through clenched jaws.

My chin drops in shock, and I continue to eat my lunch and pretend I'm not witnessing this conversation.

"Next time I will." She takes a step and then stops, turning back for the last word. "I'm glad to see you covered up my name with a new tattoo. I wouldn't want anyone to think you're still in love with me."

I drop my fork, bowled over by her remark. I search under the table trying to retrieve it. When I look up, she's gone, and Ben is sitting stoically eating his food.

Ben says very little for the rest of the meal, except to insist on paying the bill. We get into the truck, and I feel like I need to break the silence.

"You can talk to me, you know."

"There's nothing to talk about."

Typical man. "How about the woman who showed up at lunch and ruined your day?"

Ben remains tight-lipped, but I'm not giving in.

"She's the one that it didn't work out with?"

He rubs the back of his neck and ignores me. That's okay, I already know the answer. "Did she cheat on you?"

"Nope," he says turning red in the face. "If you must know, she and I dated in school. She was everything to me. After graduation, she changed."

"How?"

"I always knew what I wanted to do with my life. We didn't have a lot of money, so I took a lot of part-time jobs and apprenticeships to put me through night school so I could learn my trade. She wasn't happy with the hours I had to put in, or the lack of money in my pocket, and I felt like I was starting to lose her. I packed it all in and took a full-time job at one of the plastic factories in town."

"That still wasn't good enough for her?"

"It was for a year. I saved up everything and bought her an engagement ring. When I proposed to her, on one knee, she looked shocked. I told her I wanted to marry her and start a family."

He pauses for a moment of silent reflection. "She laughed."

"What?" I ask, appalled.

"First, she said I'd never amount to anything and I'd be stuck in that hellhole forever, making minimum wage. Then she added, she had no plans on having kids but if Hell ever froze over, she wouldn't pick me to father her children."

My heart aches for him. I place my hand on his and try to console him. "Clearly she was not the right girl for you."

"How did I not know that's how she felt? How was I so blind?"

"You're asking me? I trusted the office ho."

He glances at me with sorrow in his eyes. "I wasn't good enough for her."

"Ben, girls like that don't think anyone is good enough for them. She'll end up having several meaningless relationships and end up alone in a one-bedroom apartment with twenty cats."

I see a hint of a smile. "Looks like we both lucked out. We could have spent the rest of our lives with the wrong people."

"You're right," he finally admits, as he pulls up in front of the house and waits for me to get out.

"Do you want to hang out here for a bit?"

"Thanks, but you've got work to do, and I should spend some time looking after the business side of things. The boys will be out here tomorrow to start rebuilding the porch."

"The porch?"

"Yes, that's what I wanted to talk to you about at lunch. I know we were just going to do the bare minimum to get the place on the market, but I can't let it go. I need to rebuild that covered porch."

There's a dim light in his eyes right now and I feel his pain. I haven't got the heart to turn him down. "Okay."

"Okay?" he confirms.

"Yes." I wish I knew what to say to make things better for him.

"I'll see you tomorrow." He puts the truck in drive, and I take it that's my cue to leave. No kiss, nothing? I wait a moment, but he looks away. I get out of the truck and watch as he drives away, wondering if he's still in love with her.

CHAPTER FIFTEEN

The following morning, I'm sorting through the drawers in the kitchen and packing up boxes for donation when the door opens and Ben steps in.

"Hey," he says cautiously, feeling out my mood.

"Hey."

"I just wanted to let you know I'm sorry for yesterday."

I stop what I'm doing and glance up. "There's nothing to be sorry for."

"I wanted yesterday to be about you and I spending time together. Seeing her threw me for a loop and I acted like an asshole. I'm sorry."

"It's okay, I spent the night sorting through the stuff in this house, and I've decided I'm going to get rid of most of it."

He frowns. "Any luck finding your papers?"

"None."

"The guys are getting stuff ready to start on the porch, is there anything I can do to help?"

"Do you want to help get a load ready to take to the donation centre today?"

"I can do that." Ben crosses the room and lifts my chin with this finger and sweeps his lips across mine. "I'm over her. I promise."

I want to believe him but there's been so much deception in my life. I search his face and find sincerity there. The corners of my mouth curve into a small smile. "You can start by getting the clothes out of the dryer. They're all going."

"Are we okay?" he asks, before leaving my side.

"Yeah, we're okay." I'm not really okay, I'm leaving in less than two weeks and the closer he gets, the less I want to go.

"What do you want me to do with this pile of clothes?" he asks, as he returns downstairs with his arms full.

"Throw it in that old trunk. I'm sending it all to the second-hand store."

"Your mother's trunk?" he questions.

"Yes, it's time to put it all behind me."

Ben lifts the trunk up onto the couch as I begin to fold the clothes and stack them beside it. "I guess it's time we both put the past behind us and start looking to the future." He opens the lid and lifts the pile of clothes I've folded.

"Be careful," I warn, pointing inside. "There's a rip in the lining."

He drops the clothes back on the couch.

I furrow my brow. "What are you doing?"

"Checking it out."

"It's always been there." I cock my head to one side, "Are you working out a restoration plan? I'll go get you a needle and thread," I jest.

He scratches his head. "I don't think this is a rip, Cora, it looks like someone has very carefully cut along the seam here."

"Well, that's just silly, why would somebody do that?" Aunt Bea's words come flooding back to me, pinning me where I stand.

"Cora?" Ben says, concerned about my momentary gap.

"Is there something inside?" I ask, staring stoically at the rigid trunk and wondering if it's been right under my nose the entire time.

He squints and examines the edge of the fabric. Carefully he slides his hand under, feeling around beneath it. When he turns to look at me, his eyes wide open and brow raised, I get a nervous, sick feeling in my stomach. I watch as he gently slides a folded, discoloured document out the opening. My hand begins to shake as I reach for it then stop. "I can't. You open it."

Ben unfolds the paper and reads while anxiety rushes through my veins like crashing waves.

"Is it my birth certificate?"

He raises his eyes to mine. "It's a birth certificate from May 18, 1988. But it's not your name on it."

Feeling like my legs go limp, I sit on the couch and force myself to breathe. "What name is on it?"

"Mother's name is Allison Grace Scott. Baby; female. Margaret Hope Clarke."

Ben sits beside me.

"I don't understand. That has to be my birth certificate, but it doesn't make any sense."

"Didn't you need your birth certificate to get your passport?"

"Yes, but I was only fifteen when I took that first trip with the school to France. Nana and Pops had to file for my passport then. When I had to renew it and apply for my work visa, I obtained what they call the short version, or the wallet size." I get it out of my purse to show him.

He reads it and looks at me. "Look. Right here."

I lean in to read the small print. "Nee – Clarke." I give him a blank stare. "I've never seen that before. Does that mean what I think it means?"

Ben nods. "It means that your surname at birth was Clarke."

I begin to feel overwhelmed and my bottom lip begins to quiver. "My mother changed my name?"

"Or your grandparents did."

"Why would they do that?"

"They must have had a good reason. Maybe they wanted to keep your birth father from finding you."

"I can't believe they'd do that. Why would they try to keep him from me?"

"I don't know," he says, passing the original paper to me, "but your father's name is listed on here," he confirms in a soft tone.

I take it out of his hand and stare at it for a very long time, reading his name a thousand times over, committing it to memory: Robert Joseph Clarke.

I fold it and put it on the night table and sit in silence a few moments. "I don't know what to do now."

Ben leans in and holds his forehead against mine in silent support, then reaches over and places his hand on mine, giving it a gentle squeeze. "You don't have to do anything if you don't want to. You could just choose to look forward, and not back. You don't have to make any decisions right this minute."

I feel hopeless.

"How about we go out for a drive and get some fresh air? There's someplace I'd like to take you."

I walk with him out to the truck and climb in. "Where are we going?"

"It's a surprise, but you're going to love it."

"Compared to the last surprise, I'm thinking there's a good chance."

Ben slides on a pair of aviator style glasses and turns to give me an unimpressed look. I fix my hair in the reflection and smile.

I fold my arms in front of me, trying to keep my breasts from bouncing around and causing any injuries, as he aggressively drives his truck up the poorly graded dirt road. Ben grins as he glances over at me and I'm certain he's hitting every pothole on purpose.

"Good Lord, where are you taking me? My internal organs are going to be bruised from all this rough handling."

"We're here," he says, pulling into a partially hidden driveway.

"Milly's Roadside Farm Market?" I read as we pass a hand-painted sign.

"You're going to love Milly."

I slide out of the truck into an inch of wet muck, and hold on to the hood until I'm out of a large puddle. For a moment, I thought I was going to relive a historical moment from my childhood, while Ben almost sprints to a small wooden shack built at the front of a huge vegetable farm. Inside there are tables and shelves holding baskets of farm fresh produce and a jar at the door marked, "Honour system."

"Jake and I met Milly and her husband a few years ago. We were driving up this road, and at that time they just had an old trailer, sitting at the end of the driveway with bushel baskets on it. Jake and I started coming by for fresh vegetables, and one day Milly was out there when we stopped. We got to talking and found out that this was her way of making a little extra money to put aside for their kids' college."

"Oh, that's a neat idea. How many kids do they have?"

"Seven," Ben says without batting an eye.

I feel my jaw drop. "She's planning on sending seven kids to college on money she's making selling lettuce at the end of the road?"

"Jake and I had the same thought, so we showed up one weekend, with wood and some friends, and we built her this little shack. She's not a big-time grocery store chain, but she does okay. I don't think most people know that she's here." He gives me a sideways glance.

"Does she do any advertising?" I ask, perking up when the conversation rolls around to my area of expertise.

"I'm pretty sure that's not an expense she has the budget for. Come here." He grabs my hand and pulls me to the other side of the shack. You have to try one of these."

"A butter tart?"

"Milly makes the best butter tarts in all the counties in the Hills of the Headwaters."

"Well then." I pull a few dollars in coins out of my jacket pocket and walk over to drop them in the jar. "I need to taste them, if they're that good."

Ben takes one off the plate and unwraps it. He holds it between his finger and his thumb, so I can take a bite.

"MMMM. Raisins," I say, as I chew and swallow.

"My mother used to say, 'If it doesn't have raisins in it, it's not a real butter tart.'"

"I'm always impressed by people who can make their own pastry." I take the tart out of his hand and take another large bite. My face turns red when Ben looks at the size of the bite, and I read his unvoiced thoughts about how wide I can open my mouth. "Don't even say it," I warn.

"I wouldn't dare."

I take the last bite and lick the crumbs and sticky filling off my fingers. "Mmmm. My grandmother made amazing pie crusts. On more than one Christmas she tried to teach me how. She stood behind me and supervised, step by step, but somehow my pastry always came out flat and hard like roofing shingles."

Ben laughs.

A voice from outside the window startles us. "I recognize that laugh. Is that you, Ben McCarthy? Are you here eating my butter tarts again?"

A buxom woman enters the vegetable hut, smiling. Three children who look to be under the age of seven follow her in.

"I am! And I brought a friend. This is Cora Scott."

She reaches out to shake my hand. "Sorry to hear about Bill, honey. He was a good man. We thank the Lord he's no longer suffering."

"Thank you."

Ben unfolds a twenty-dollar bill and stuffs it into the glass jar. "Nothing better than a home-cooked meal with farm fresh vegetables," he says, waggling his eyebrows.

"I think you're my biggest fan," she says blushing.

I raise my hand. "I'm a fan of your butter tarts."

"That recipe has been in my family for years," she says smiling.

"Don't even bother asking for it," Ben advises. "She won't give it up."

"Well, that's disappointing."

"Go on, now. You've got better things to do than hang around here all afternoon."

Ben grabs a bag of potatoes, lettuce, carrots, and beans. I watch, amazed as he stacks it and manages to get it all the way to the truck without anything falling. He's clearly done this before.

"You should have warned me I'd need my boots," I scold, as I use his running board to scrape the mud off my shoes before I get in.

"You should know it's rubber boot weather at least until the end of June."

The drive home goes too quickly. I'm enjoying the fresh air and Ben's company. I haven't thought about France all day. Ben turns the truck into the driveway and then slows to a crawl. "What the fuck?"

"That's odd," I reinforce when I see what he's looking at. "How did he get over here?" I wonder out loud, as I look at Gordon the garden gnome, sitting in the opening of a hollow tree stump at the curve on the driveway.

Ben's forehead puckers. "Did you move him?"

I shake my head. "No." I stare at him, making sure his painted brown eyes don't follow us, as we drive past. "I told you, strange things are happening around here."

"What's going on at the barn?" Ben asks.

I take one last look at the gnome, ensuring he's still in the same place. "I don't know, let's check it out."

Jake is standing outside the barn door, with my car pulled halfway in and looking very frustrated.

"What's happening?" Ben asks as we get out of his truck.

"I was going to send Caleb to gather up all the wood you piled up out back, but I can't get this old farm truck started."

"So you called Dad?"

"Hi, Phil!" I holler when I see him coming out of the barn with jumper cables.

"Hi, Cora, you look beautiful today. The country air agrees with you."

I feel myself blush. There is no disputing the family resemblance between the men. They all have the same rugged jaw and dimpled smile. Jake is just a little bit taller with leaner muscle. Ben tosses him his keys. "Here, just take my truck."

I laugh, and he looks at me confused. "What's so funny?"

"That Chevy is not gonna make it back up that hill with these puny little wheels. The ground is too soft still."

Ben ignores the chuckles from his family. "Well, then we'll have to wait another day."

"Or... I can start the Ford."

His shoulders shake with laughter. "If Dad and Jake couldn't get it started, what makes you think you can? You can barely keep your own vehicle in running condition."

My face turns red as he painfully reminds me of my shortcomings. I pivot quickly and grab a hammer off the hood of my car. I warn Ben off with a hard stare as I walk past him into the barn. They follow me in and watch, arms crossed and legs shoulder-width apart, waiting for me to fail. I lift the hood, then turn to look at the boys, raising my brow. "Well? Somebody get in the truck!"

Phil climbs in and waits for my cue. I glance over at Ben and catch him shrugging his shoulders in silent communication with his brother. I climb up on the bumper and hang over the engine. "Turn it over," I yell.

Phil turns the key, and nothing happens except the 'click.' I smile and wield my hammer. "Try again! But don't give her any gas." This time, as it clicks, I tap the starter with the hammer, in small but deliberate strikes. "Again!" I yell, with my hammer ready. The starter chortles, bringing her back to life, and he quickly revs the engine to settle it into a healthy idle. Ben rubs the back of his neck. "Well, fuck."

I slam down the hood with a victory smile. "Do you think I lived on this farm all those years without learning how to keep the equipment running?"

Ben throws his hands in the air in surrender.

"Marry this girl," Phil suggests, as he climbs down out of the cab.

"That would be hard since she's planning on living in France," Ben retorts.

I feel my face turn red and I search for a comeback, but my phone rings. I take a few steps away to answer it. The boys busy themselves with the truck until I end my call and turn to look at them, distraught.

"What's wrong," Ben asks, concerned.

"Aunt Bea collapsed this morning. She's in the Intensive Care Unit."

CHAPTER SIXTEEN

"Thank you, for going with me to see her," I say, fidgeting with my phone on the way to the hospital.

"Of course. I wouldn't let you go alone." He reaches over and picks up my hand, brings it to his mouth, and kisses it. "When you care for someone, you show up. That's how it works."

When he releases my hand, I brush the pad of my thumb across his cheek and along the cut of his jaw. My emotions bubble close to the surface. "She's all I have left."

"No, Cora. You have me, and you have Jake and Dad. You're not alone in this world."

Until I go back to France. My muscles tighten and I feel tense.

"When I called this morning, they said they moved her from the ICU into palliative care. It didn't sound like that was good news," I share as he parks in the hospital lot.

Ben holds my hand as we walk toward the main door. "Well, it means that she's stable."

"But she's not going to get better."

"We don't know that for sure. There's a chance she could bounce back if she's not ready to go."

I hesitate before entering her room. Ben stops behind me and squeezes my shoulders. I step to the side, to make room for a nurse who's leaving with the blood pressure machine.

"How is she doing?" I ask.

"She's tired but in good spirits."

I look at Ben, alarmed. "It must be bad, if she's in *good* spirits."

"Maybe it's the meds," he reasons.

The nurse looks at us confused.

"When will she be able to go home?"

She gives me a sympathetic smile and reaches up to rub my elbow. "She won't be going home. She's comfortable here, and since it's only short term, they've decided to let her stay until..." She pauses and decides not to finish her sentence when she sees the look of horror on my face. "We'll take good care of her," she promises.

I push back the curtain and walk in slowly. "Aunt Beatrice?" I call softly so as not to startle her. Her eyes flutter open and I feel a huge sense of relief. She gives us a weak smile.

"How do you feel?"

"Very tired, dear."

"You gave us a bit of a scare yesterday."

"That caregiver of mine is always exaggerating things."

"Mhhm, she was exaggerating. That's why you spent the night in intensive care."

"I was fine there," she argues. "Then they moved me to geriatrics, and there was so much yelling and commotion going on, I thought I was a prisoner of war. Fucking old people."

Ben turns away, his shoulders shaking with laughter.

"Do you feel up to visiting?"

"Yes. Help me sit up so I can see you."

Ben plays with the button, raising the head of the bed; then the foot; then both simultaneous. I raise my eyebrows. "Stop it!" I mouth. He gives me a boyish grin and adjusts her into a sitting position.

"There. That's better, now we can see you." I take the remote out of Ben's hand and move it to the other side of the room to take away any temptation.

"Aunt Bea, I have a very important question to ask you."

"Hopefully I'll have an answer. I'm ninety years old, you know. My memory isn't what it used to be."

"Clearly, because you're only eighty."

"Really?" She waves her hand dismissively. "It doesn't matter much. The good thing about a bad memory is I make new friends every day."

Ben and I share a look and smile.

"We found a birth certificate hidden in the old travel trunk."

"You did? That's wonderful. I knew it was hidden somewhere in that house."

"Do you know who Margaret Hope Clarke is?"

She smiles and reaches for my hand. "Why, that's you. Before Maggie changed your name."

I glance over at Ben and he nods his acknowledgment. "Do you know who changed my name?"

"That was Margaret. You were barely four years old. She convinced my brother, it was the right thing to do to change your surname back to the family name."

"Do you know why?"

"I only remember that she felt guilty."

"Guilty about what?"

"Keeping secrets," she says in a shaky voice.

"About what?" I press, in frustration.

"Cora," Ben interrupts. When I look at him, he shakes his head, indicating he thinks I'm pushing too hard.

I soften my tone. "Auntie, do you know who Robert Clarke is?

She squints her eyes trying hard to remember. "Was he the mayor in 1953?"

"No, I don't think so." I'll try a different approach. "Do you remember my father's name?"

Her face brightens. "Yes, I do remember now. It was Robbie something. He seemed like such a nice boy. Handsome too. He reminded me of my James. I think he was visiting for the summer. He was your mother's first love. Maggie didn't like him. She was afraid he was going to take Allison away from her. She just couldn't lose the only child she was blessed with." Tears come to her eyes. "She lost her anyway."

"What secrets did Nana keep?" I ask again.

"The boy never knew Allison was with child. Maggie made sure of it."

"How?"

"She took all of her letters out of the post box. They never got sent."

I look at Ben, thunderstruck. "Did Pops know about that?"

"No, Maggie was good at keeping secrets. She confessed to me, just before she died, and asked me not to tell him. She felt what happened was all her fault and she didn't think Bill would ever forgive her for it." She begins to weep, and I reach over to hold her hand.

"Why wouldn't she want me to know my father after my mother passed away?"

"I remember now. She was afraid he'd come back and take you away. She didn't want to lose you too."

Anger builds inside me; I can feel it eating at me.

A nurse pops her head in to check on Aunt Bea's rising blood pressure. "I think she needs to rest now."

I nod, trying to calm myself. "Aunt Bea, we're going to come back and visit you soon." I get to my feet and lean over her, kissing her on the forehead. As I straighten to leave, she reaches out and grabs my hand. "She loved your mother, more than anything in the world. And after she was lost, she loved you the same."

A tear escapes from my eye as I gently pull myself away.

"I'm sorry," Ben says as we walk back to the truck.

"Just when I think I've found out the worst of my family secrets...Bam...Plot twist!"

"Well, at least you're getting answers now, that must help some?"

"Very little, right now."

"I suppose it will take some time to set in and understand."

"Or I can just block it out of my mind and tell everyone I'm an orphan and don't know anything about my family history."

I don't know whether I should scream or cry.

"Listen, would you mind if I make a stop at the general store before we go home?" Ben asks, ending my pensive silence.

"No, if you need to, I'll be fine."

"Have you ever been to the general store in Hockley?"

I shrug. "I don't think so."

"It's an amazing place. You're going to love it."

It's a beautiful winding road through the hills to the village of Hockley. My anger and sadness begin to fade along the away.

The homes and vintage trucks here are perfectly preserved in time. I can see why Ben likes this town; I'm captivated by its charm before we even get out of the truck. I don't know what to look at first as we cross the road to the building that appears to cater to many of the locals needs. "There's a liquor store?" I say surprised.

Ben holds the door open for me and grins. "That's what I'm here for. You're out of beer."

"Do I need beer?"

"You never know when someone might drop in."

I laugh. It's hard not to. "You and Jake are the only ones who drop in."

"And...we drink beer."

I gasp as I step inside the store and look at him with amazement. Shelf after shelf is stocked with beautiful gifts and décor for sale.

"A lot of the locals sell their merchandise here."

I walk past a selection of fresh-baked goods and treats. "Milly should sell her butter tarts here."

Ben smiles. "I like the way you're starting to think."

"There's even a coffee bar," I say amazed as Ben pays for his beer.

"People drive up from the city to go hiking or golfing, skiing in the winter. Some of them drive up here, just to shop in this store. There are so many amazing bed and breakfasts in the area for people to stay at."

"What a wonderful place," I admit as I buckle my seat belt.

"That's what I've been trying to show you, Cora. People come to the Hills of the Headwaters for its beautiful landscape and friendly communities. The surrounding counties are growing and changing, and a lot of our local businesses have embraced this new blended culture of city glam and small-town country charm.

I'm suddenly aware that this is an effort to convince me to stay in Mono Mills. "Wow. That's some campaign speech. You should run for mayor."

"Tease me, if you want. You know exactly what I'm getting at; you made this point to me the other day. There are dozens of shops like that country store throughout our surrounding counties that could be thriving, but nobody knows they exist. And if some of our older family businesses don't learn how to promote themselves in today's market, they'll lose everything."

I stare out the truck window at all the small business signs at the end of driveway lanes on our way back to the house. Lawnmower repair, scrap metal, roofers, and driveway paving. Everyone is trying to make ends meet. It would be a great challenge; I reason with myself. I look over at the man sitting beside me. If nothing else, he should be the reason I stay.

"Wow!" I exclaim as we pull up to the house.

"What?"

"Nobody's here."

Ben chuckles. "I guess they all went home."

"It's so...quiet."

"Enjoy it while it lasts," Ben says with an odd timbre in his voice.

My phone rings and I open my eyes wide. "It's my boss."

"Okay, I've got a couple things I can do outside."

"Thank you," I say quietly as I connect the call. Ben looks like he's up to something, but I don't know what. "Hi, Marion."

"Hi, Cora, I just read through the project update. Things look like they're going well."

"They are. Did you receive the documents from the advertising department?"

"I did. I liked them. I did have a few suggestions. I just emailed them to you."

"I'll review them and send you any changes."

"Great! So we're on schedule and I'll see you next week?"

"Yes, absolutely."

"Great. I knew you wouldn't let me down."

I open my laptop and sign into my email while I say goodbye and end the call. I sit at the table, concentrating so intensely on her suggestions that I don't hear Ben come back in.

"Still working?"

"Just responding to an email," I say, still looking at the keyboard.

"I need you to *unplug* and put it away for a while." He puts a plate on the table in front of me.

"What's this?"

He lights a birthday candle in the middle of one of Milly's butter tarts.

"It's a birthday celebration."

"It's your birthday?"

"Nope, my birthday isn't until August."

I open my eyes wide. "Oh, you're a Leo! That explains a lot."

"Very funny. I realized yesterday when we found your birth certificate that your birthday was the day of your grandfather's funeral."

I look downward.

"Since Gretchan wasn't here with you to plan a birthday party, I just assumed there wasn't much of a celebration that day. So I planned one for tonight."

I give him a half shrug. "It's just a day. And his name was Et-i-enne," I enunciate.

"Whatever. The guy is a dirtbag. I really don't care if I pronounce his name properly. And...it's certainly more than just a day. It's a day to party and celebrate with our friends."

"I don't have any friends, Ben."

His eyes sparkle. "Are you sure about that?"

The door flies open and Jake barges in. "Hey! Hope you're both decent. I'm here for the party!" He drops a case of beer on the floor.

"What party? There is no party," I insist.

The door opens again, and one by one the guys who've been helping work on the house step in.

I narrow my eyes at Ben, and he shrugs innocently. "Looks like a party to me." He leans in and whispers in my ear, "I'm sorry, Cora, I know it was a rough day for you, but they've been looking forward to it all day, so I didn't want to cancel. I'm hoping you're okay with it, but if you're not up to it, just say the word and I'll ask them to leave."

I look around the room at all the smiles and realize I'm surrounded by laughter and friendship. The house is loud and bright and cheerful. "I think I could use a little fun right now."

He hits me with a quick peck on the lips. "That's my girl."

A stack of pizzas gets plopped on the kitchen counter, and before I even know what's happening in my own house, there's a hockey game on the television, a poker game going down on my dining room table, and a sing-along happening alongside a blazing bonfire. There's so much commotion I don't know where to start. Ben does the rounds with me, introducing me to the girlfriends and wives of the guys I see here every day. It's nice to sit and chat with female companions for a little while. Since I've been home, my only visitors have been the all-male construction crew, and there have been few conversations at the house that didn't eventually come around to the topic of someone's flatulence problems or penis prowess. I glance up from my conversation and catch Ben staring at me, his eyes full of mischief. I wave and he waves back. With a grin, he nods his head in the direction of the patio door.

I make my way across the room, stealing the bowl of popcorn off the coffee table as I pass. "Nice moves," he says, as I meet him at the door.

"What do you have in mind?"

"I need a little quiet time. Follow me."

Quietly, he pulls back the sliding glass door and we escape.

"I miss the sound of the frogs in the evening," I say, as we take a walk down to the pond, spilling popcorn along the trail.

"You know, most girls wouldn't know that sound was the frogs singing." He stops to skip a stone across the water.

"Well, I'm not just any girl. I was born and raised in the Hills of the Headwaters."

The moon shines brightly, reflecting on the water. "You're practically royalty."

There are times in our relationship when Ben and I compete for power, and there are times we walk side by side, as friends and equals. Lately, there are times, like right now, when the pure feminine entity inside me craves his dominance. He senses it, moving toward me like a lion on a hunt and warning me he's about to take things up a notch. Instinctively I retreat, stepping back until my back presses against the trunk of a large willow tree, and I can go no farther. He yanks the popcorn bowl out of my hands and tosses it into the nearby bulrushes. Holding my attention with a ravenous gaze, he cages me in. My thighs clench together, and my body vibrates with anticipation.

"You are so beautiful in the moonlight." He lowers his lips to my neck and nibbles his way to my ear. I can feel the rapid rise and fall of my chest as he pulls my shirt to the side to expose my bare shoulder. Gentle kisses, mixed with hard nips of his teeth, have me squirming with need. I reach down to unzip his pants and he grabs my wrist, stopping me.

"Not here," he whispers. "There's too many people roaming around."

I hear giggles coming toward us. "They probably followed the trail of popcorn," I say with a simper.

"Up there," he motions, as the voices get closer. "In the barn." He holds my hand and guides me through the dark, using his cell phone as a flashlight. Once we're inside, he latches and locks the door, preventing any surprise visitors. "Now, where were we?"

He brushes his fingertips across my cheek and rakes it through my hair before closing his fist. With gentle pressure, he forces my head back and growls obscenities as he explores my body with his lips, starting at the nape of my neck. "I really want you naked right now."

My hands explore his heavily muscled body, craving the feel of his bare skin. "I was just thinking the same thing."

In a few heated moments, clothing is strewn around the barn and we are both completely naked. Ben moves his body against mine, and I caress my hands over his bare chest. He stops me, taking my hands and holding my wrists tightly as he pins them over my head, forcing me back against the cold metal door of the vintage Ford. He consumes me with a hungry kiss, deepening the passion as his tongue slides inside. The chill of the evening air, and cold metal against my back, makes me shiver. Still in an attentive mind, Ben stops. "Get in the truck." He pulls open the door and holds out a hand.

It's an authoritative command I dare not ignore. Without hesitation, I climb into the truck cab and try to make room for us both on the bench seat. Ben caresses my body, leaving behind a warm trail where his hand explores. Forcing my knees apart, he strokes between my thighs until I'm dripping with need and moaning. In a flash of a moment, I'm on my back, and Ben is on top of me. With each stroke he presses me down into the bench seat, consumed by his driving need. He sucks my nipple into his mouth and teases it with a hard pull. I sense his release bearing down on him, and I try to circle my hips, searching for the pressure I need to join him, but my position restricts my movement. I growl in frustration. Ben withdraws and pushes himself back onto the seat. Addled by his action, I try to sit up and protest. I can tell by the look in his eyes, he's not done with me yet. Pulling me onto his lap, he positions me to straddle him. He lowers me gently, concentrating on a careful penetration. It feels so good, I become distracted by my own need, and grind against him until my sensitive knot of nerves begins to tingle. I raise myself, almost to the point of withdrawal, and Ben grabs my waist, stopping me. I tighten around him and sink all the way down. Ben grips my hips and guides me, repeating the movement and increasing the pace at which our pelvic bones slam together hard. Waves of pleasure wash over me, starting small and increasing in size, my body begins to tremble as I meet my explosive release. Ben is quick to follow and jerks his hips in one last orgasmic spasm. I collapse exhausted against him, trying to steady my thundering pulse.

Perspiration dampens my skin. Ben strokes my hair and caresses my back until I feel a chill as the heat of our bodies begin to fade. "We should get back to the house. They'll be looking for us."

"I'm pretty sure everyone sitting around the bonfire knows where we are," he chuckles.

"I didn't know you were a screamer," I tease.

"I'm pretty sure it was you who screamed out."

"That's not the story I'm going to tell if anybody asks."

He gives me a quick slap on the ass.

"Ouch," I squeal.

"Get your clothes on."

"I can't believe I just had sex in my grandfather's truck," I say, hopping on one leg, trying to put on my pants.

Ben pulls his T-shirt over his head. "I'm pretty sure you're not the first person in your family to have sex in it."

I looked at him appalled. "Take that back."

He shrugs.

"I can't even believe you would put that thought in my mind. What's wrong with you?"

CHAPTER SEVENTEEN

I wake up in the morning, on a mattress in the back of Ben's pickup bed. I struggle to sit up and take a look around. There are a few vehicles still parked in the driveway and Jeff and Steve are still sitting on logs at the fire.

"Good morning!" Jeff hollers when he sees I'm awake.

Ben lifts his head and reaches for me. "Come back to bed, it's too early."

Steve sneaks around the side of the truck with a long blade of grass and tickles Ben's nose with it.

"What time is it?" I ask, searching for my phone.

With his eyes still closed, Ben's hand flies through the air, grabbing the grass and pulling it out of Steve's hand. "It's an asshole past too many beers o'clock," he mumbles.

Watching from the fireside, Jeff bursts into a fit of laughter. When Steve returns to the fire, he picks up a twig that's been dangling over the rocks and hot coals. "Want some breakfast?" he asks, holding a blackened charred wiener in the air.

My stomach turns. "No, I'm good. Thanks anyway."

I pull down on the bottom of my T-shirt and fix my bra.

Jeff snickers as I tug at the blanket tangled around us, trying to get free. "It got a little chilly when the fire died down, we covered you up," he says.

I look down at the unfamiliar item. "Where did you get this blanket from?" I ask suspiciously.

"Out of the back of Gary's truck."

My head snaps up, startled. "Gary the horse breeder?" I quickly toss that blanket to the side and ignore the immature giggling from the two drunk men.

"Where you going?" Ben asks, peeking through one eye.

"I have to pee."

"What's in your hair?"

I run my fingers through my curls and discover a sticky wad of something. I look at it on my fingers, feeling disgusted. "Dear God, I hope that's marshmallow."

Steve laughs hysterically until his face turns red and he wheezes trying to get air. He composes himself a moment, then in a second fit of laughter, he holds his stomach as his knees come up to his chest, causing him to tip backward off the log and land in the dirt with a thud.

I gasp. "He's not laughing anymore, is he okay?" I ask as I get down from the truck.

Jeff walks over and stares down at him and gives him a little kick with his toe. He looks at me and shrugs. "He's snoring, so I guess he's fine."

"Are you just going to leave him there?" I ask on my way into the house.

"I'll let him sleep until the guys come back to finish the porch."

I can't disguise the look of shock on my face. "You're going to work today?"

"Yes."

"You have got to be kidding me."

He shrugs. "We made a commitment to get this job done before you leave next week."

His comment stalls me. The time has gone by so fast. "I'm going to put a pot of coffee on before I take a shower, help yourself when it's done. Help yourself to several cups of coffee maybe."

I can see the back porch door is open when I come down the stairs after my shower. Ben is sitting, reading the paper, drinking a cup of coffee.

"Good morning."

"Hello, beautiful," he says in a gruff voice.

I blush and it seems to please him.

"I was going to join you in the shower, but you locked the door."

"We still have company roaming around. I was afraid I'd end up with an unwanted visitor."

He tilts his head slightly. "Probably a good call. I was wondering, would you mind if I didn't go with you today to visit Aunt Bea?"

"Feeling a little rough, are you?"

"Nah, I'm okay. There's a project I want to get done today, and I want to make sure the place gets cleaned up."

"Another secret project?" I kiss the top of his head. "No worries, I'll be fine."

"Message me when you're on your way home."

"I will."

I pull out of the driveway in what I'm now referring to as my vintage automobile. I saw that tag line on an ad when I was researching what I should sell it for. As I back up and turn the car around, I stop and look to see if anybody is around. Gordon, the gnome, is now sitting on a log over by the fenced-in chicken coop.

"How did you get over there?" I wonder aloud.

I use the time on the drive to the hospital to reflect on my life and all the things I've learned about my family, and our past. I just reassured my boss that the marketing campaign is going well, and I'll be in Paris to deliver our ideas successfully to the client in a week. All I can think about this morning is that Ben won't be there with me for the biggest pitch of my life, and I want him there. I'd be lying to myself if I didn't admit part of me doesn't want to leave Mono Mills at all. It's starting to feel like home again.

I meet Lynn in the hallway, on her way out. "She's not having a good day," she warns me.

"Oh, well I won't stay long. I just want her to know I'm thinking about her."

Lynn smiles. "Just remember, she's not quite herself. Take nothing she says to heart."

Sensing she's already said her last goodbye to Aunt Beatrice, I wrap my arms around her and squeeze her.

"Thank you, for being so kind to her. It can't always be easy. I don't think I could do your job. I'd be an emotional wreck."

"It has its ups and downs. Mostly ups. I don't think I'll ever get used to this part. I've already been reassigned to a new client who needs help; I start tomorrow. If I don't see you again, please take care of yourself and have a safe journey back to France."

"I will and thank you again."

Aunt Bea's eyes are closed when I enter the room. I don't want to wake her. I sit beside the bed for some time, watching her sleep. She begins to cough and opens her eyes, looking around the room frantically, as if she doesn't know where she is. I get to my feet and reach out for her hand. "Aunt Bea," I say loudly. "Aunt Bea, I'm here."

"Allison?" she says blinking her eyes.

"It's me, Cora. Allison's daughter."

"You're not Allison?" she asks, confused.

"No. Allison is my mother. I'm Cora."

"Where are we?"

"We're at the hospital."

"Can I have some water?"

I look around the room and find a glass by the bedside. I help her sit up and get the straw into her mouth to take a few sips.

"Thank you," she says as I lay her back gently. "I was talking to James before you came in."

I blink my eyes, at a loss for what to say.

"You were?"

"Yes, he comes to visit me every day."

"Oh, that's nice of him." I suppose the only thing I can do is play along.

"Pass me my lotion."

I search for it in her belongings and take the lid off.

"My skin is so dry, and James loves the smell of lilacs."

I look at the purple label and smile as I put a small dab in the palm of my hand. "So do I." The flowery fragrance fills the room as I rub it on her arms and hands.

"Do you know where I put my Sunday hat?"

I glance over at a small overnight bag that holds few personal belongings. "No, I'm sorry. I don't."

She gets visibly upset. "I need to find it; he wants me to wear it when I see him again."

I feel myself becoming emotional. "I'm sure it will turn up soon."

"My hair is probably a mess," she exclaims.

"I can brush your hair for you, if you like."

Her eyes close. From the long pause in conversation, I'm certain that she's fallen back to sleep. I dab a tear from my eye and occupy myself with straightening up the room. I open the closet, in search of her hat, even though I doubt most of her personal items have accompanied her here.

"Allison? Are you still here?"

I sit on the side of the bed and take her hand, no longer concerned about correcting her. "Yes, Aunt Beatrice. I'm right here."

"Promise me you'll forgive your mother. It's important you forgive her," she says, becoming upset. "When you practice forgiveness, you let go of the hurt and anger in your heart, and you make room for love. Love is very important. Promise me, Allison."

The words catch in my throat. "I will, I promise."

She lifts her head, quite urgently and startles me. "You wouldn't lie to an old woman on her deathbed, would you?"

"Of course not," I insist.

She smiles and lays her head back down on the pillow. "Good. Then we can all be a happy family again."

I weep in the elevator on the way down to the first floor, and by the time I reach the car I'm sobbing uncontrollably. I take a few minutes to pull myself together before I call Ben.

"Hi?"

"Are you okay? Sounds like you've been crying."

"Yeah, I'm okay. You thought yesterday was bad, today was really hard."

"Do you want me to come get you?"

"No. I'm on my way. I'll be there in ten minutes."

"Okay, drive safe. When you get here, park down by the hollow oak tree and honk. I'll come get you."

"What? Why?" I protest.

"You'll see. I know it's hard for you, but can you just do what I ask?"

I consider it. "I don't know, I guess we'll see."

I do as he asks and put the car in park halfway up the driveway, by the old oak tree, and honk. He walks down to meet me.

"How is she?"

"Fading fast. She didn't even know who I was today. She kept calling me Allison."

"That's tough. I'm sorry."

"What are you up to?"

"Just wait and see."

"See what?"

He takes my hand and walks me up the hill to the front of the house. As it comes into view, I glance over at him, bewildered. "Is that the original front door?"

"No," he says apologetically. "I wanted it to be the original, Cora. I tried hard to restore it, despite the rot, but it was too far gone. I used the original hardware and some of the trim. Jeff matched the paint colour and we found a door that Jake salvaged from an old farm up north that was similar."

"Oh, Ben. It's wonderful," I say, walking over to it.

"I was hoping you'd like it."

"I do." I reach out to touch it. "It's so much better than that ugly aluminum one."

"I agree."

"The colour is perfect. This door looks like it belongs here. I wouldn't have known it's not the original. You could have lied to me,"

He furrows his brow. "Why would I do that?"

I shrug and look away.

"Hey, look at me." He lifts my chin with his finger. "I promise, I won't ever lie to you. No secrets, no twisted truths."

I gaze into his green eyes, and I want to believe him. I turn the handle and push but it won't budge.

"Well, that was a little anti-climactic," I say under my breath.

"Here," Ben says, approaching from behind. He gives it powerful nudge and it pops open. "We're going to fix that."

I walk through it, and stand on the other side feeling happy, like I did when I was a small girl. "It's a perfectly wonderful surprise. Thank you."

CHAPTER EIGHTEEN

I open my eyes in the morning, wrapped in Ben's arms.

"Thank you for staying the night with me."

"You didn't sleep at all."

"I've got a lot of things on my mind."

"I can tell."

"I promised Aunt Bea that I'd forgive Nana for the lies and deceit."

"You did?"

"She thought she was talking to my mother at the time. But still."

"I can't imagine how hard this is."

"I understand that Nana didn't want to lose my mother, but I was so angry when Aunt Bea told me she kept me a secret from my father, even after my mother died, because she was afraid of losing me too."

"It's hard to come to terms with choices other people have made when you can't talk to them and understand their actions or reasons."

"Aunt Bea seems to think she acted out of love. As selfish as that seems. Originally, she was scared she was going to lose my mother; then she was afraid she was going to lose my pops if he ever found out what she did. She said Nana told her she regretted her decisions, every day for the rest of her life."

"And you have your doubts?"

"No. But I can't help feeling the way I feel. I don't know if that will ever change."

He tightens his grip around me. "Well, you can be angry and resent her for the rest of your life, or you can forgive her and start healing. I vote to move forward and concentrate on the future."

"It's sounds easy. I'm not so sure it is."

"How can I help?"

"I honestly don't know."

He nestles his face in the nape of my neck. "What are you going to do about your father, now that you have his name?"

"I don't know. Finally fill out the family tree?"

He laughs once and kisses my shoulder.

"Ben?"

"Yes."

"Would you ever consider moving to France?"

He brushes his fingers through my hair. "My family is here. My brother and dad need me."

"You've never wanted to leave everything behind and live somewhere else?"

"Mono Mills is my home, Cora. There is nowhere else for me."

"What if everyone you loved was gone? Would you still stay?"

"It's hard to say for sure until you're in those circumstances, but I think so."

I pull back the covers and sit on the side of the bed. "What if the one that you love lives someplace else?"

Ben rests on his elbow. "Are you asking me to go to France with you?"

"No."

His expression saddens and I avoid looking at him while I get dressed. "I was just wondering."

"Where are you going?"

"Downstairs. I've got work to do."

"I'll be down after I have a shower."

I open my laptop and review the corrections made by the graphic design team, based on Marion's suggestions. She was right on the money; I guess that's why she's the big boss. A little idea starts to wiggle into my brain and I open up a bunch of tabs and start to build a new campaign.

"Are you still working?" Ben asks, sneaking up behind me and peeking over my shoulder.

I jump. "Kind of," I say embarrassed, tilting the screen to try to hide what I was working on.

"Wait a minute, let me see what you're doing."

Despite my objection, he flips up the screen and looks at my work. I wait for his censure.

"I thought you were doing work stuff."

"I was."

"This doesn't look like a high-profile Parisienne project," he teases.

"Well...I started to. Then I started to think about Milly and her kids, and what you said on our way home from Hockley. Even a social media campaign would help create some awareness of her business in the community." I look for his approval.

"You're definitely right about that. It would help."

"Simple stuff, like Facebook and Twitter; Instagram. Things the older kids can help her with."

"Makes sense. You're a good person." He presses his lips to the top of my head.

"I think I'll pop in and show it to her."

"I'll go with you," he says, putting on his shoes. "The painters are showing up today to freshen up the inside of the house, so it's probably a good idea if we're out of the way."

"Shouldn't one of us be here?"

"Jake's on his way to Mount Forest to do some salvaging, but Dad will be here."

"You guys really are close."

"We are. We depend on each other."

I glance at the chicken coop on the way out the driveway and notice the empty log. I look all around, trying to find him, but he's nowhere in sight.

"What are you looking for?" Ben asks, crinkling his forehead.

"Nothing."

We turn at the cross road and start heading north when I get an anxious feeling, like I'm being pulled in another direction. We pass the road sign for the cemetery, and I feel warmth on the side of my face, as if someone is whispering in my ear. I pull my hair over it and try to take deep calming breaths, but a few more moments down the road and I'm riddled with an anxious energy. I can't shake it. There's something I need to do.

"Ben, would you mind if we stop at the cemetery first?"

He doesn't question me, just puts on his blinker and changes course, pulling over to buy a bunch of flowers from a neighbour's roadside stand on the way. We park at the south side of the property; then Ben gets out and rounds the hood of his truck. Before I even get my seat belt off, he opens my door, showing me his chivalrous side. The sun isn't warm enough yet to have completely dried the morning dew, and it makes for a slippery climb up the hill. He extends his hand and uses his strong biceps to support me.

"Look," I point out the patch of recently overturned soil. "Pops is here now."

I have an emotional moment as I stare at the new marble gravestone that has both of their names on it.

"I don't know where to begin."

Ben hands me the bouquet of flowers. "Just say what's in your heart."

I place the bouquet of flowers on Nana's grave and pause. I swallow hard and nod.

"Hey, Pops, I hope you don't mind but I need to have a word with Nana." I pause, as if I'm waiting for an acknowledgment. "Nana, I'm sure when Pops arrived, he gave you a proper hello. I understand how terrifying it must have been for you, thinking you were going to lose the people you loved the most. I'm not gonna lie. I was pretty angry that you kept the truth from me all these years." I reach down and take Ben's hand. "I think I'm starting to understand that once you've experience someone's love, it's hard to imagine living life without it again." He squeezes my hand.

I lower my head and whisper, "I don't want to spend the rest of my life being angry. I want to let go of the hurt and make room for love." Ben leans in and presses his lips on the top of my head. I take a stuttered breath. "I forgive you, Nana."

A gentle breeze brushes past, and I close my eyes and smile as I place my hand where I feel a warm kiss is pressed against my cheek.

"Those flowers are really fragrant," Ben notes.

I inhale deeply and then open my eyes. "I don't think that's my flowers," I say, looking down at the wildflowers I placed on her grave. "I smell roses."

"That's odd," Ben agrees.

The hair on the back of my neck stands on end. I stiffen as I force myself to look to my left.

"Cora?" Ben says, concerned.

I take a small step toward the man standing at a grave in the distance, then hesitate. I glance at Ben over my shoulder and take a few more steps. He acknowledges the stranger and follows a few feet behind me, giving me space, but ready to act if needed. It feels like the walk takes me many years before I finally arrive where he stands, in front of my mother's grave. He doesn't acknowledge me at first, just stares sadly at the fresh bouquet of roses he's placed at the base of the grave stone. I finally find my voice. "It's a lovely morning."

"Yes, it is."

"Those are beautiful roses."

He doesn't answer but I persist, "Did you know her?"

"A very long time ago," he admits sadly.

Neither of us diverts or eyes from the gravestone. I can feel my heart pounding in my chest like a hammer. I quickly glance over at Ben for courage, and he provides me with a nod of encouragement. "Is your name Robbie?"

He scrubs his hand over his face, looking uncomfortable. It makes me nervous. "Robert," he affirms with a Scottish brogue. "Have we met before?"

"I've been wondering about you." The words get stuck in my throat. "I'm your daughter," I say in a quiet, shaky voice.

He turns to look at me, and tears well up in brown eyes that mirror my own. "You're my daughter?"

Unable to speak, I nod my head.

"I didn't know about you all these years."

"I didn't know about you either. I've been trying to find out who you were." It feels like someone is squeezing my heart so hard it hurts.

"I didn't know," he repeats.

I nod my head, trying to reassure him. "I have so many questions."

A pained expression washes over him.

"I can't."

"I understand," I lower my head, disappointed as my eyes fill with tears.

With his fists clenched at his side, Ben steps forward. "Listen, buddy, she's been through a lot the past few weeks. I won't take it too kindly if you brush her off without giving her some answers."

He shakes his head. "That's not it at all. I have somewhere I have to be this afternoon." He reaches into his pocket and finds a scrap of paper and continues to search for something. Ben reaches into his back pocket for a pen and hands it to him.

"Thank you," he says, as he scribbles something on what looks like an old receipt. "Give me a day or two, I have to take care of a few things, then call me. I promise to answer all your questions. I just can't do it today." He stares into my eyes, then reaches out to brush a tear from my cheek. "You look just like her."

I watch in silence as he walks away. Ben wraps his arms around me from behind and holds me close. When my father gets to his car, he pauses, looking at me for a long time, before he lifts his hand, gives me a single wave, then leaves.

"Can we go to Milly's another day?" I ask, as I climb back into Ben's truck.

"Of course."

"I don't feel much like visiting today." Ben turns on the radio and I raise my brow at the sad country song playing. He gives me an apologetic look and changes the station, each one, worse than the last. "I'll just turn this off."

"Good plan."

There's a flurry of activity at the farm when we get back. "Where did all these people come from?" I ask.

"I hired subcontractors to do some of the painting. We were getting behind schedule, and we've only got four days until you leave."

The reminder is like a slap in the face and I look at him frazzled. "Is it that soon?

He nods. "You are still leaving, aren't you?"

I give him a reluctant nod.

"Just thought I'd check."

"Is that Caleb painting the barn?"

"Yes, with his new friends."

"Jeff says things have taken a turn for the better."

"That's really good to hear. You had a lot to do with that."

"Like I said...there's no such thing as a bad kid. Why don't we walk the property and see how things are coming along?"

I'm impressed with the progress and how much better everything looks with a fresh coat of paint and a good cleaning. I stop at the old apple tree with the tire swing hanging from one of its limbs. Ben tugs on it to gauge its sturdiness. "I think we should take it down; I don't think that branch is strong enough, and I don't want anyone to get hurt."

"Nonsense," I announce, backing onto the tire and sitting down.

"Be careful," he warns.

I wave at Phil as he watches us from the house and then push with my feet to get it swinging. "See?"

"I see, but it still makes me nervous." He watches the branch bend under the stress. I place my feet on the ground, with the intention of giving myself another push, but before I can say another word, Ben grabs me and pulls me to safety as the branch comes crashing to the ground.

I shrug. "Oops?"

"Enough fun and games, I want to show you what we were working on all day."

As we approach the house, I'm awestruck. There's a roof over the porch that frames the front of the house. The scrolled wooden trim has been restored and painted white, and in the middle of it all the tangerine door welcomes us. Just as it always did when my nana was alive.

"Look!" I yell. "There's Gordon! Sitting in the garden."

"Isn't that where he belongs?"

"Yes, but every time I see him, he's in a different spot."

"What do you mean?"

"One day he was by the tree, then he was over by the chicken coop."

"That's curious," Ben says.

"I told you what my great-grandfather said. Gordon is the guardian of the farm, I'm sure of it."

"You don't say? Hey, Jake!" he yells.

Jake looks up and walks over to us. "What's up?"

"Have you noticed that gnome doing anything... suspicious?"

He looks over his shoulder. "That gnome?"

"Yeah."

Jake gives him an odd look. "No. We've moved him from time to time, like you asked, so he didn't get trampled on while we were working."

I cross my arms in front of me and Ben starts to laugh. "Thanks, Jake."

He looks annoyed. "Can I go back to what I was doing?"

"Sure."

Jake walks away and looks back at us a few times, shaking his head.

"Did you think Gordon was wandering around by himself?" Ben asks playfully.

"You're an asshole."

A horn beeps behind us, and we turn to see the SUV pulling in. "Hi," Fiona says out the open window. "The place looks fantastic."

I look around at the property and see the home I remember. The tree where I read books and the butterfly garden; the porch where we ate too much strawberry shortcake.

She opens the door and gets out. "I was driving by and figured I'd stop in. I'm glad I did. I think we can sign some papers."

"Papers?"

"Yes, you've got a lot accomplished here, and I think we can confidently get you some more money."

"But we still have a lot to do," I reason.

"That's okay, you can keep working on them. We can sign the listing papers right now and get it on the market, but we'll hold off any viewings until the weekend. You're leaving in a few days, right?"

I suddenly find it hard to breath and I look at Ben.

"Good, let's go in the house and make things official. Then you don't have to worry about it, I'll look after everything from there." She walks toward the house and I hesitate, feeling panic-stricken.

Ben reads my hesitation as doubt and as I take a step to follow, he grabs my arm to stop me. "It's not too late to change your mind."

Emotional turmoil churns inside me as I stare at him, wondering how my life would change if I stayed.

"You can make ends meet, here," he insists.

My heart sinks. "You know, you've made a lot of pitches over the past few weeks, trying to convince me the community needs me, and that Mono Mills is my history and my home. But not once have you asked me to stay for *you*."

He stares at me but remains silent. Heartbroken, I shrug out of his grasp and follow Fiona into the house.

CHAPTER NINETEEN

Ben is absent from the property the following day. I desperately needed to hear his voice last night but when I called I went straight to voicemail. Every time Jake comes into the house for something, I feel awkward. I busy myself with boxing up the last of my grandparents' belongings, feeling like my heart is in a million pieces.

Caleb comes into the house to fill his water bottle. "Hey, buddy."

"Hi."

"Can you help me get a few things down off one of the shelves in the cellar?"

"Sure."

He follows me down into the dark, damp basement and climbs on the bottom shelf.

"Careful, I don't know how sturdy these shelving units are."

He stretches to his limit and gets a hold of the last item, a box marked preserves, and pulls it toward him. I scream as it comes crashing to the ground. It hits the floor with a thud, causing Caleb and I to look confused.

I tip it over and a stack of letters, bound with an elastic, fall out. I know instantly what I've just discovered.

"Are you okay, Cora?" Caleb asks, concerned at my silence.

"Is everything okay?" Jake yells from the living room. "I heard you scream."

"Yes, I'm fine." I reach the top of the stairs and tuck the stack of mail inside my carry-on. I'll have several hours on the plane to decide what to do with them.

"Where's Ben?" Caleb asks Jake.

"He's working on another project." Jake looks at me, but I avert my eyes. The heaviness in my chest is almost unbearable.

"We're almost done here. It's customary for the client to inspect the work and sign off."

"I have no complaints about your workmanship. I'll make sure to give you a raving review."

My phone rings, and Jake walks around looking at the few remaining pieces of furniture in the house, while I listen to the caller.

"What are you doing with these things?"

I disconnect the call and drop my phone on the table. "The agent felt it would be better to leave some furniture in the house for showings, but it looks like that won't be necessary."

Jakes chest expands with air and he gets a hopeful look on his face. "Have you decided to stay?"

I frown. "No, Jake, that was Fiona. She already has a buyer who's interested in the house."

"That was fast," he says, looking disappointed.

"Yeah, it was."

"Where are you going?"

"I have to go and see Milly before I leave."

This time, I wear my boots.

"Are the older kids home?" I ask.

"Yes, they just got off the bus."

"Great." I open my laptop. "Let's get started."

I'm amazed at how quickly they pick up the concept of advertising on social media. Even Milly seems to have a good handle on it.

She follows me out to the car. "Have you heard from Ben?" she asks me sympathetically.

I'm always shocked at how quickly news spreads in the country. "No, I haven't."

"It's a shame you have to go. Seems to me you two are good for each other. And you both deserve to find love."

"I guess it just wasn't written in the stars."

She gives me a look and I know she sees right through my bullshit. "Sometimes, Cora...you just have to grab the stars by the balls and decide your own destiny."

I throw my arms around her. "I'm going to miss you, Milly."

"You're going to miss my butter tarts," she corrects.

"Can I have the recipe?"

"Not a chance," she says as I get into the car.

"I had to try, one last time."

She stands at the end of the drive and waves until I'm out of sight.

When I get home, the tradesmen are packing up their tools and cleaning up the debris. I search the property hoping to catch a glimpse of him, but Ben is still nowhere to be seen.

I guess choosing my career was the right choice. I put the finishing touches on my ad campaign and sign off on the design departments paperwork. Everything is falling in line and ready to go for my presentation.

I sold my car for a few hundred dollars and rented one to drive myself into the airport tomorrow. All I need now, is to sell this house.

Emotionally drained, I sit at the dining room table, anxiously waiting for Fiona. I finally convince myself that I've made the right choice, since Ben isn't around with his constant sales pitches, confusing the issues. Clearly the past few weeks meant nothing to him. When I'm at work, I'm focused and unemotional. It may be busy, but my career is *uncomplicated*. Since I've come home, I feel like my life is in turmoil.

I haven't slept for two days, because every time I close my eyes childhood memories come rushing back to me, trying to anchor me emotionally to this house. No matter how hard I try to break my ties here, there are reminders in every nook and cranny of this home and the surrounding property. And I miss Ben. I try to deny it, but I do. This house has felt empty without him and unless I take Milly's advice, it's about to get a whole lot emptier.

I jump out of my skin when Fiona lets herself in and closes the door.

"It's your lucky day," she says cheerfully, as she drops her stuff on the table and pulls out an orange folder. "I've got an offer and good, but there are a few things the buyer would like to include in the deal."

"Give them anything, I really want to get this over with. I fly back to France tomorrow."

"Okay, but as your agent I need to go over them with you. First, the buyer has agreed to our asking price."

"That's good, isn't it?"

"Yes, but he's asking that we include the ownership to the farm truck in the back barn and all the farm equipment, tractors etc."

"Nothing runs."

"His request to include these items states that he will take possession *as is*."

I truly don't think that any of it has any resale value. I think on it a minute and conclude my moment of apprehension is only because I can't imagine anyone other than my pops working this land with them.

Fiona jumps in to prompt me. "At least it would spare you the expense of having everything towed away to the wreckers or the dump...or wherever old farm equipment goes to retire."

"I suppose the best place for everything is here, if the new owner wants it. I'll agree to that."

"Next, the buyer would like some of the furniture that still remains in the house. There's a list." She passes it to me, and I read through it, wondering why anyone would want these pieces."

"This stuff is worn and half-assed repaired. I was going to burn it all before I leave."

She shrugs, "One man's treasure, as they say. Again... *as is.*"

I'm dumbfounded as to why anyone would want the old cedar chest and a desk with a broken drawer. They had value to me because they belonged to my grandmother, but it's hard to believe that to anyone else it would be anything more than junk. I remind myself I need to cleanse myself of sentimental possessions and move on. "Okay, they can have everything on the list."

"Great! Then you just sold your property."

I furrow my brow. "That was easy."

"That's the way we like them," Fiona adds, as she marks a bunch of places on the paper for me to sign.

"When will the offer be firm?"

"As soon as you sign it." She slides the paper across the table.

"I thought there were things that had to happen. Conditions to be met."

"No conditions on this one, honey. This man knows what he wants, and he understands what he's getting. He wants immediate possession, so you can go home tomorrow...if there's no reason for you to stay."

Our eyes meet and I look away. I know exactly what she's hinting at, and I want to avoid any conversation about it.

"I'm still confused."

"There are no conditions on finance, the buyer's mortgage is approved. There is no house inspection, because he already knows what work has been done and what's left to do. One more," she points at the box she marked with an X.

I initial the box I missed.

"And…" she flips to the last page. "Sign your name, here."

I ready the pen and hesitate, looking around the room at all the memories I'll be leaving behind. Tears well up in my eyes, and I'm afraid if I don't sign it quickly, I'll change my mind. I pen my name on the line marked seller, then glance at the signature on the other side of the page. My heart stops. I read it again and then look up at Fiona, shocked.

A smile blooms on her lips. "He's waiting outside."

I open the door to see Ben leaning against the hood of Fiona's SUV. His hands in his pocket and ankles crossed. My heart beats faster. He stands erect when he notices me approaching. When we stand face-to-face there's an uncomfortable silence.

"Why?" I finally manage to speak.

He shrugs. "You need the money, and I think this place has a lot of charm and potential."

"What's your angle?" I ask. "You're going to fix her up and flip her for a profit?"

He raises a brow. "Flip it? No! Why would you think that? Not everybody you meet has an angle, Cora."

"Maybe not, but it feels like it. So, it wasn't me you wanted? It was the house," I say emotionally.

He takes a step toward me and takes my hands in his. His expression makes me anxious. From the moment I met him, he has always portrayed himself as a strong confident man. Whatever is going through his mind, right now, has him terrified. *I'm* feeling nervous for him and I don't even know why.

"Not at all. Turn around."

He halts my protest before it starts. "Please, just turn around."

I turn to face the house and Ben moves closer, pressing himself against me, and wrapping his arms around me from behind. I sigh, realizing at that moment just how much I missed his touch. "What do you see?" he asks.

"Is this a trick question?"

"Humour me."

"I see an old worn-out, broken-down house."

"What else?"

"A door, painted an obnoxiously bright shade of orange."

Ben squeezes me tighter and lowers his cheek to the side of my head. "I see a home. I see family, young and old, coming together for Christmas dinners. I see a little girl, excited to see her grandfather, when she gets off the school bus at the end of the lane. I see a dog, chasing chickens around the property."

My heart begins to race. "That was a long time ago."

"This isn't the past I'm talking about, Cora. I'm looking to the future."

I glance over my shoulder at him.

"What are you telling me, Ben? You're going to live here?"

"I am." I feel a sudden tension in his body. "And I'm hoping I won't be living here alone. I see my future here, *with you*, Cora."

I feel like all the air just left my lungs. "Ben." My emotions bubble to the surface and try to cloud my rational thoughts. "I have a job, in France. An apartment."

He presses his lips to the side of my head. "I know you think your life is there, but it's not. HOME is behind that tangerine door. Behind that door your grandparents created a home full of love. It can still be that. With you and me."

"Apparently my grandparents' life was not all sunshine and roses," I remind him.

He spins me around to face him. "Is anybody's? I'm not saying that there won't be struggles. There's gonna be burnt dinners and clogged toilets."

"Unpaid bills and arguments over money," I add.

"You stood up at your pops' funeral and said you had a happy childhood. You said your grandparents were rich because of family and friends and *this* community. Were you lying to all those people who loved your pops?"

"No!"

"Picture it...I'll come home after a long day of fixing stuff, and smile when I get to that tangerine door, because I know on the other side of it, children will come running, happy to see me."

I raise my brow, shocked.

"And you'll be there to welcome me home with a kiss, and later once the kids are asleep, we'll steal some time alone together down by the pond. And we'll be happily in love, growing old together, on that very front porch where we'll read to our grandkids."

Tears stream down my cheeks. "I want all those things, but they're just lies."

"No, they aren't. We can have all the things your nana said would be behind that tangerine door. We can find happiness. We can find hope. We can find love."

He gently wipes the tears from my cheek with the pad of his thumb.

I'm torn between the career I've been working so hard for and the feelings I have for Ben. But he still hasn't said the words I need to hear. My heart feels heavy.

"Why? Why do you care so much about me?"

"Why do you find it so hard to believe that I do?"

"I'd spend the rest of my days looking after you, even if I hadn't promised your pops I would."

My eyes open wide, and Ben pauses, realizing what he's just said.

"You promised my grandfather you'd look after me?"

"Yes."

"I didn't know you even knew my pops that well." I can feel a defensive wall going up. "Why would you never mention that conversation to me?"

He shrugs. "When he got really sick, we used to stop by to check in on him."

"We?"

"Jake, my dad, and me"

"And you used to talk about me?"

"Not really, Cora. He told us about you and how worried he was you were going to be alone."

"And so you volunteered for the job of what? Savior? Protector? Babysitter? FRIEND?" I say angrily.

"NO," he argues. "It wasn't like that. He knew he was dying, and you would have to come home, and he asked us to make sure you were okay." He softens his tone. "To make sure you didn't have to go through it alone."

I feel my body stiffen and my fists clench tight. "You made me a promise. No lies; no deception."

"I didn't lie to you. I just didn't tell you about it."

"I think that falls under the category of twisted truths. All these things you've done for me, all the time you spent with me, that was a lie. You didn't do it because you cared for me. You did it because you made a promise to an old dying man."

"That's not true. Don't be angry."

"Don't tell me not to be angry," I scream. "People have been lying to me all my life."

"Okay," he says in a gentle tone. "You're right. I should have told you we used to visit him. But I didn't do all those things because I promised him."

"Why did you do them?"

He reaches for me, and reels me in. "I did them because I love you. I knew it from the minute I pulled you out of that broken-down car, wearing your designer clothes and smelling like French perfume."

Finally, he says the words, but I pull away. "I don't believe you."

"You can ask Jake or my dad. You don't think they would lie to you, do you?"

I pause, confused and hurt. "I don't know what you want me to say."

"Say you'll stay; say you love me," he pleads. He searches my face and his eyes cloud with heartache. "Say I'm good enough."

It feels like I've just taken a knife to the heart. I shut down.

"Do you love me, Cora?"

Yes, yes, I do. Just tell him. I take a step back, putting some space between us. "It's not that easy," I say, feeling the weight of my emotions starting to bear down on me. "I need time to think." I can't stand still; I pace like an angry animal. Five minutes ago, I was ready to stay, but how can I trust that there will be no more lies after his confession? I don't think it matters that I love him; he just convinced me I've made the right decision.

Ben purses his lips, and his expression hardens. "For fuck's sakes, Cora. It's not something you think about. Love is something you feel. You either feel it or you don't."

I can't tell him I love him. The words get caught in my throat, as if saying them out loud will condemn him to some kind of horrible curse. A lifetime of darkness, tragedy, and death to all who Cora Scott chooses to love.

Tired of waiting out my pause, he nods, taking my silence as his answer. "I see."
I feel like I'm about to make the worst mistake of my life. Still, I let him walk away, without speaking a word. When he gets into the SUV and slams the door, I wipe away my tears and go back into the house.

"You don't look happy," Fiona says, appearing disappointed. "This isn't what you wanted?"

"Of course, it is," I say sarcastically. "Who wouldn't want to meet a guy like Ben and fall in love, only to walk away and leave it all behind?" I wipe my nose and establish eye contact with her. "Please don't ask me why I'm leaving."

"It's none of my business." She gathers up her stuff and frowns.

"I have to arrange to ship a small container of stuff to France. When do I have to have it out of here?"

"We put the closing date for a week from now, to give the lawyer time to get it done. I'm sure if you need more time, Ben won't mind it being here a bit longer."

I stare out the kitchen window at the SUV. "I wouldn't be so sure of that. Tell him he can move in right after I leave tomorrow."

CHAPTER TWENTY

I stop by the hospital on my way to the airport to say goodbye to Aunt Beatrice. She wakes for only a few moments.

"Maggie says you forgave her."

"I did," I say, ignoring that she's still talking to dead people.

"I'm proud of you, Cora." She smiles before she closes her eyes again. I'm glad she knows who I am today. I kiss her on the forehead and say my goodbyes.

I feel distressed as I drive out of town. I'm not just running away from the feelings I have for Ben, there are answers to questions about the past that still haunt me. It eats at me, all the way out of town, and when I pass the Caledon town sign, I pull into the gas station and make a call.

"Hello."

"Hi," I say nervously. "Mr. Clarke. It's Cora. Cora Scott." It dawns on me that he may not know my name. My hand trembles nervously. "We met at the cemetery."

"Please, call me Robert."

"Robert," I say awkwardly. "I know this is really random, but I'm on my way out of town, and I was wondering if you were free to meet with me for a coffee?"

"Right now?"

"Yes, I'm sorry. I'm on my way to the airport. I've decided to return to France and I…"

"Now is fine. I'll text you the house address, if that's okay. I'm babysitting my granddaughter, and they didn't leave me a car seat. You'll have to come here."

"Oh." The thought of having half-siblings and a niece unnerves me. I hadn't even thought about gaining other family members when I found my father. "If you're sure it's okay."

"Yes. I've been thinking about you a lot. I'd like to see you before you leave."

A young child starts to fuss in the background. "I'll see you soon." I drive across the road and pull into the drive-thru. By the time I pay for the two coffees, his address shows up in my messages, and I copy and paste it into my GPS. He's only two minutes up the road.

I swallow hard as I pull into the driveway. I turn off the key and sit frozen for some time, wondering if this is a good idea. I suppose I can't call Ben and ask for his opinion. After the way we left things, I couldn't even bring myself to call and say goodbye. I look up and see Robert standing at the front door, with a small child on his hip. Now that he's seen me, I can't change my mind and leave.

He welcomes me into his home, and we settle in the living room with our coffee.

"Sorry for the mess," he says, kicking a path through the toys meant to entertain the toddler. "My son got called into work and his wife had an appointment to get her hair done so I offered."

"That's okay, this was a spur of the moment visit."

"I'm glad you called."

I smile at the toddler; her brown eyes and curls are familiar. "I have a brother," I acknowledge.

"Yes, his name is William."

I narrow my eyes.

"No coincidence. Your grandfather was the hardest working, most decent man I knew."

I'm curious about the connection. "Robert, how did you come to know my family?"

"I was born in Scotland. I didn't know my own father, he died when I was baby. My mother did the best she could to raise me on her own. She ran herself ragged, trying to deal with a rebellious teenage boy, on the verge of becoming a man, so she shipped me off for the summer to live with my grandparents in Mono Mills. They owned a farm not too far away from William and Maggie."

"They were neighbours?"

"Yes, they were. I was a bit of a challenge for my aging grandparents, but William saw something in me and gave me work for the summer on his farm. He worked me to exhaustion, but everything I learned about being a good man, I owe to Bill Scott."

"And my mother?" I ask softly, trying not to push.

A smile curls at the corner of his mouth. "I remember the first time I saw her. She was sitting on a stump down by the pond, painting. I fell in love with her the first moment she looked at me with those blue eyes. She had this way of looking right through me, past all the piss and vinegar. She was the kind of love a fella never forgets."

The small girl climbs up on his knee with a blanket and a bottle and leans against his chest. He cradles her, lovingly stroking her hair, and holding her like she's a precious treasure. Jealousy briefly creeps over me; I wish I had known these moments as a young girl. "I'm trying to understand why my mother..." I take a breath and frown, deciding against directly asking the question. "What happened that summer?"

"It was a hot one, I remember that. Your mother and I fell deeply in love. We spent a lot of time hiding out in that old barn, away from the world. Summer came to an end, and my grandparents decided our place was with my mother, so they leased the land and packed up everything else and moved us back to Scotland."

"You left?"

"Yes, I was only sixteen at the time, but even after all these years, I consider leaving her behind the toughest thing I have ever done. I tried to convince Bill I could take care of her, but Maggie insisted that taking her with me to Scotland wasn't an option she'd consider. Bill and I struck a deal. I go home, stay out trouble, and finish school to prove to him that I'd become a good man. Then, and only then, I could come back to work on the farm the following summer. If all went according to plan, he'd consider giving me full-time employment the following year when I graduated."

"You planned to come back?"

"Yes, I didn't want to go. I was going to come back as soon as I could. My grandparents still owned the land, I could stay there and work with Bill until he agreed to let her marry me."

"I don't understand, if she knew you were coming back why was she so..."

"Sad? Two years felt like a lifetime to your mother. She was angry at Bill and Maggie, accusing them of trying to keep us apart. The night before I was supposed to leave, she drove over to my grandparents' farm at three in the morning in that old farm truck and threw rocks at my window until I woke up. She had packed everything she owned in a big old trunk that she could barely lift on her own and talked about running away and getting married."

"I still had that trunk until recently. I kept it all these years."

"Is that so?"

"Obviously you didn't run off and get married."

"No. Lord knows I was tempted. I thought about it more than once. I put her in that truck and drove her back home. I pulled it into the barn, and we stayed together there, all night long. We were young, and in love. Emotions were running high and one thing led to another..."

Ben was right! We weren't the first. My eyes open wide and I wave my hands, stopping him right there. "You don't need to finish that thought. I know where you're going, and I don't want the details."

His ears turn red. "In the morning, I walked home, and we left for the airport. I never saw her again." He wipes a tear from his eye, and it pulls at my heartstrings.

"Your mother was a talented artist, with a lot of potential. She was hoping to go to art school and graduate with a degree. It would have been selfish for me to ruin that for her. I thought I was doing the right thing."

"I found a letter, inviting my mother to attend one of the most prominent art schools upon her graduation from high school. I ruined those plans. Because of me, she didn't finish school at all." My bottom lip begins to tremble.

"No, Cora. I ruined those plans. She never forgave me for leaving her."

"How do you know that?"

"They didn't have cell phones or high-speed internet back then and long-distance calling was expensive. I wrote her a letter every week and mailed it. She never wrote back. Not once. It gutted me. I figured she never wanted to see me again, so I cancelled my plans to return, got a job in Glasgow, and moved on without her."

He lifts the sleeping toddler and places her gently on a blanket in the bottom of a playpen. When he returns to to his seat on the couch, I'm pulling a stack of elastic bound envelopes out of my bag. His brows draw together as I hand them to him. He flips the edges, looking at the handwritten address on the unopened letters and his eyes begin to get misty.

"I found those, hidden in a box in my grandparent's cellar. Seems my nana had a talent for hijacking the postal deliveries."

Robert gives me a confused look.

"I don't believe my mother knew about these letters. I think my nana thought she was protecting her by hiding them from her."

I see a pained expression on his face. "She thought I had forgotten about her?"

"As you're telling me your story, I'm beginning to think so. And there's something else you need to know. Some of these letters are from you...and some are from my mother, to you."

His head shoots up in surprise.

I pull the envelope from the bottom of the pile and double-check the date on the postmark. "This is the first letter she wrote to you, after I was born."

He turns it over and finds it still sealed. "You didn't open it."

I shake my head. "I thought about it, a million times, but it didn't feel right because it's not addressed to me. You should be the first one to read it."

He carefully pries open the flap and slides out the letter. As he unfolds it, his hands slightly tremble, and a photograph falls free. I place my hand on his knee and give it a firm squeeze.

My dearest, Robbie.

It's been nearly a year since you left. I miss you so much my heart hurts. I had hoped to hear from you after I wrote that we were expecting a child. At times, I have experienced such unhappiness that I didn't feel like I had the will to live without you. My father reminds me that you are busy, trying to finish school and working part time to support your mother. I know you have to prove to him that you

can take care of us, so I will keep hope I will soon be with you again. I'm writing to you today to let you know we have a daughter. I named her Margaret, after my mother. This tiny little blessing is the most beautiful of all my creations. She gives me a reason to live. She has your chocolate brown eyes and button nose. I took this picture for you, so you can keep it with you until you can meet her in person.
With all the love in my heart, until we can be together again.
Allison

He lifts the fallen picture so we can both see, and tears stream down my cheeks as I realize it's a copy of the picture Ben found in my mother's room. When Robert breaks down and sobs, I throw my arms around him and squeeze him tightly. Barely holding it together myself.

CHAPTER TWENTY-ONE

The door opens and we both look up startled. A tall handsome young man stands at the doorway, looking uncomfortable. "Everything okay, Dad?" he asks concerned.

Robert gets to his feet and pulls himself together. "Yes. William," he says, nervously clearing his throat. "This is Cora. I told you about her; she's my daughter."

He extends his hand and then understanding flashes across his face. "My sister."

"Apparently," I say nervously as I take his hand.

"Crazy world this is. Father just told us that he learned about you. I was wondering if we would get to meet you."

I notice a slight hint of Scottish brogue. "I'm on my way to the airport. I'm going back to France today."

"Oh, that's a shame. I'll get the squirt out of here and let you guys finish catching up."

"She's very beautiful."

He holds the limp toddler like a rag doll and grabs the blankie and bottle with one hand. "Thank you." He pauses. "I hope you keep in touch. My wife is dying to meet you. She's going to be pissed that she wasn't here."

Robert smiles, and closes the door behind them, before coming to sit beside me again on the couch. He stares at the stack of envelopes. "What are you going to do with them?"

"They belong to you. I'm going to leave them here."

"I'm not sure my heart can take reading them. The pain she must have been in, thinking I abandoned her."

"My grandmother carried that guilt with her, after my mother died. That's why she legally changed my name to Cora."

"Cora was your mother's favourite art teacher," Robert recalls. "She's the one who sent her work into the art institute and helped her fill in the application."

I pick up the letters and stack them on the table. "When you're ready, maybe I can visit, and we can read them together."

He nods and exhales an anxious breath.

"I know this is a lot to take in on one day, but can I ask when you found out about my mother passing away?"

"I didn't know, for many years. I figured she'd moved on. When my grandparents passed away in Scotland several years ago, I inherited the property in Mono. I always loved it here, and I had an opportunity to transfer my job. I came back to see the place before I decided. One night, I drove past Bill's farm, and I could see him working up by the barn. I was a very happily married man, with my own family by then, but even after all those years I couldn't get her off my mind and I had to know how she was doing.

"It was then that Bill told me about the tragedy around her death. At first, I was heartbroken; then I was angry that nobody told me. I had lived all those years wondering if she went to art school or had fallen in love and was happily married; if she ever thought of me."

He looks at me, frustration darkening his face. "And then the guilt set in. I couldn't sleep, I couldn't eat. I couldn't get it out of my head that she was dead because of me. If I had gotten on a plane and come back when she didn't reply to my first few letters, then none of this would have happened. I was afraid to come back and have her break my heart face-to-face."

I rub his shoulder sympathetically.

"The whole time, she was waiting here, thinking that I didn't love her, and she took her own life."

Tears roll down my cheeks as I experience my own gut-wrenching heartache.

"When a friend told me where she was buried, I drove up there and wept for hours at her graveside. I returned home to my grandparents' farm that night and decided to put it on the market the very next day. I couldn't stand the thought of living there anymore." He pauses and stares at me a long while, and then throws his arms around me in a possessive hug. "Please believe me that I didn't know about you. I don't understand why Bill didn't tell me about you. I would have searched for you."

I sigh. "I don't think he knew about the letters either. He may have thought you did abandon her."

"Or maybe he felt everyone had suffered enough."

"But you knew about me when I met you at the cemetery."

He nods and gets to his feet to retrieve a large manila envelope from the other room. "A few days before you and I ran into each other, I received this in the mail." He dumps the contents on the table in front of me. "Go ahead," he encourages.

I pick the papers up slowly, afraid of what other family secrets I was about to uncover. "It's a copy of my birth certificate."

"And a copy of the legal name change application," he adds.

"What's this?"

"It's a copy of the legal documents filed by your grandparents requesting legal guardianship of you by reason of abandonment."

"Oh. And this just arrived?"

"Yes. It was postmarked weeks after your grandfather's funeral."

I detect a faint hint of a familiar scent. I lift the papers to my nose and inhale. "I think someone wanted us to find each other, so I wouldn't be alone in this world. She's the only person Nana confided in before she passed away, and I'm betting she came across these recently in a box of stuff she took from the house."

A sparkle returns to Robert's eyes. "It couldn't be Aunt Beatrice?"

"Oh, it could."

"She's still alive? Is she still feisty as ever?"

"She's alive but failing fast." I frown. "I should get on my way to the airport."

I try to ignore the look of disappointment on his face. "I think we've both had enough emotional turmoil for today."

"I feel like I've found, then lost you again in the same day," he says in an emotionally strained voice.

"I promise, I'll keep in touch."

"Come back and visit, any time you want."

"I will, thank you. This is a beautiful house, how long have you lived here in Caledon?" I lift my coffee cup to finish the last mouthful before I leave.

"A few years. The farm sold quickly to a widower who used to farm on the other side of the county. He was looking for land for himself and his two boys."

I choke and spit coffee everywhere. Alarmed, Robert gets to his feet to pass me a napkin. "Are you okay?"

"Yes, I'm fine," I say, drying my mouth and everything around me. "I'm glad it didn't shoot out my nose. That would be embarrassing."

He chuckles. "I really wish I had the opportunity to know you better before you leave."

"I wish I didn't have to leave."

"Why are you then?" he probes.

I fidget nervously, trying to think of an answer.

"I see." He gives me a knowing look. "And what about the bodyguard that was with you at the cemetery? Do you love him as much as he loves you? Or is that the problem?"

"I'm afraid."

"Of being in love?"

"No...Yes."

He reaches up and holds my arms and locks me in for a serious message. "Cora, if I could go back in time, I wouldn't leave. I'd give anything to go back and make a different decision. There's not a day that goes by that I don't miss your mother. I saw the way that man looked at you. Don't make the same mistake. Don't get on that plane."

"I can't just quit my job and move back here."

"Why?"

"I sold the property."

"Was the property the only thing worth staying for?"

I struggle to find an answer. He releases my arms. "I'm sorry. But what would your grandfather tell you to do right now? Do you think, after watching his daughter suffer, he'd want you to be unhappy? Because you will be. Work might keep you busy for a time, but eventually you're going to regret leaving him. A job is just a job, Cora. Finding someone to love, who loves you back, is *everything*."

Those words echo in my mind as I make the drive to the airport. My world has been an emotional roller-coaster ride since I returned to the Hills of the Headwaters. The only time I felt peace was when I was in Ben's arms. I'm going to miss the lush green rolling hills of home and all the wonderful people in the surrounding communities. I try to steer my thinking toward all the positive things I'm going back to in France, despite my effort I can only think of a few.

As I enter the complicated cement maze of roadways into the airport a dark, heavy, oppressive feeling comes over me, making me sense that somebody is with me in the car. As I spot the sign for the car rental return, I'm startled by the appearance of a monarch butterfly fluttering its wings and trying to land on the front windshield. One turns into two and in a split moment, there is a swarm of them blocking my view. I panic and throw on the windshield wipers, trying to frighten them away as I pull over to the side of the road and stop.

It's my mother. I know it. I feel it. She shows me imagines of Ben and his family, and she fills me with feelings of love and hope. Memories and dreams flash through my conscience guiding me to where I belong. When the heaviness lifts, I know the experience of having my life flash before my eyes.

Shaken, I merge into the main flow of traffic out of the airport and get on the highway back to Mono Mills.

I make a call to my boss as I drive. "Hi, Marion."

"Hi, Cora, I thought you'd be on a plane on your way home by now."

"There's been a change in plans."

"Oh?"

"Yes, I'm not going to make it for the presentation. I'm staying home. I'm sorry, I know I'm letting you down, but it's a good campaign and anyone can pitch it."

"I see. Is there anything else?"

"Yes, I'd like to send you a proposal to work for you as a consultant. From here. Part time."

"He must be one hell of a man," she says.

"He is."

"Well then, I'll look forward to your email, and offer to consult. You do good work, I'm sure we can come to an agreement."

I smile, feeling like I've finally made the right decision. I dial Ben's number. I don't know what I'm going to say when he answers, if he even does.

I'm almost home and Ben is still not answering, I hang up and call Jake.

"Cora? Are you okay?"

"Yes, I'm fine. Where is he?"

"What's wrong?"

"Nothing's wrong Jake, I'm coming home."

I can hear Phil express his happiness in the background. Jake laughs. "He's out at your farm."

"Thank you!"

"Go get him, and don't put up with any of his shit."

"I won't"

I rip up the road in double time, throwing up loose gravel and dust. When I pull up to the house, the tension in the air around me lightens and I'm able to breath. There's a feeling of peace wash over me, as if the spirit or spirits with me finally feel absolved of their guilt and pain. I get out of the car, my eyes darting from one end of the porch to the other. From the smallest wooden details to the bright tangerine door, it looks exactly like it did when I was a child.

I search for Ben, but the house is in darkness. I hear the door to the chicken coop slam shut and I start to walk in that direction, shaking nervously. His pace slows when he sees me, and he puts down a box he was carrying. I stop walking, unable to read his expression and fearful of his reaction.

"Hey," I say, feeling him out. "What's in the box?"

"Chicks." He crouches down to lift the flap of the box.

My heart begins to race as I watch them flit and climb and chirp around the crowded box.

He gets to his feet. "What are you doing here?"

I shrug, nervously. "I'm coming home."

He crosses his arms over his chest. "Why?"

I feel my bottom lip begin to quiver. "Because I love you." There's a long pause and I start to panic. "I don't expect you to believe me," I begin. "And I understand if you want me to leave." I'm startled as he closes the distance between us in one large stride. His lips collide with mine in a passionate kiss that sets us ablaze, and anchors us together, from our hearts to the very depth of our souls.

He finally lets me up for air, and my eyes flutter open to see a mischievous smile curling on his lips. "What?" I ask, suspiciously.

"I knew you couldn't resist me."

I laugh. "Yeah, well it's your Irish charm."

"I knew it." He takes my hand and begins to walk toward the house.

"Welcome home."

"Mono is the *heart* of the headwaters after all."

He grins and squeezes my hand tightly.

"There are a few things we need to talk about," I advise.

He stops dead. "Don't tell me you don't want chickens. I already named them."

I smile. "I'm fine with chickens...and kids, someday. It's the comment about burnt dinners and clogged toilets."

"Oh?" he says surprised.

"I'm going to have a very busy marketing career here, so you better learn to cook, and I'm not unclogging any toilets."

"Fair enough." He continues walking toward the porch. "I'll just build us an outhouse down by the pond."

It feels good to laugh again. "I talked to my father today."

"You did?" he asks, surprised.

"He's from Scotland. I can't wait to tell you about him. Oh, and I have a brother and a niece."

Ben stops at the bottom of the porch step and looks alarmed. "Wait. Back up a minute...if we have daughters, they'll be half-Irish, half-Scottish?"

I raise my shoulders. "Seems so."

He lowers his lips to give me another kiss. "I can't wait. When they become teenagers, we'll send them to live with Jake."

As I climb the porch steps toward the tangerine door, a warm lilac-kissed breeze brushes past me, and I swear I hear the muffled laughter of a young woman behind me. I slowly glance over my shoulder to see her standing by the old oak tree where I like to read. I'm not afraid at all, I feel love and I feel hope. She smiles and blows me a kiss before waving goodbye. My eyes dampen with tears as I wave, and I watch her open a brightly illuminated door that appears out of nowhere. In a blinding flash, she's gone. I take a deep breath.

"Cora? You okay?"

I turn to look at Ben and smile. "I'm better than okay."

"Good," he says, as he holds open the door.

I glance back at the old tree, hoping for one last glimpse, but there's no one there.

"Ben."

"Yes?"

"Unpack the checker board and be prepared to get your ass whooped."

EPILOGUE

On the other side of the brightly illuminated door, a young woman steps through and into a sunny, warm meadow. She squints her eyes, becoming accustomed to the sunshine. Feeling a little confused, she looks down at her dress and then lifts her hands to touch her head, adjusting her Sunday hat. She spots Bill and Maggie sitting on a red and white checkered cloth, laughing and enjoying a picnic. Monarch butterflies flutter around Allison as she stands at an easel with her paintbrush, waiting for a brown-eyed gnome to decide on a pose.

Everyone looks up as the door closes.

"Look! Beatrice is here!"

A handsome young man, dressed in his Sunday best, stands waiting with a bouquet of flowers. When she extends her hand to him, he lifts it to his lips and gives it a chivalrous kiss. He lifts his gaze to hers and smiles. "I've been waiting. Welcome home."

The Headwaters

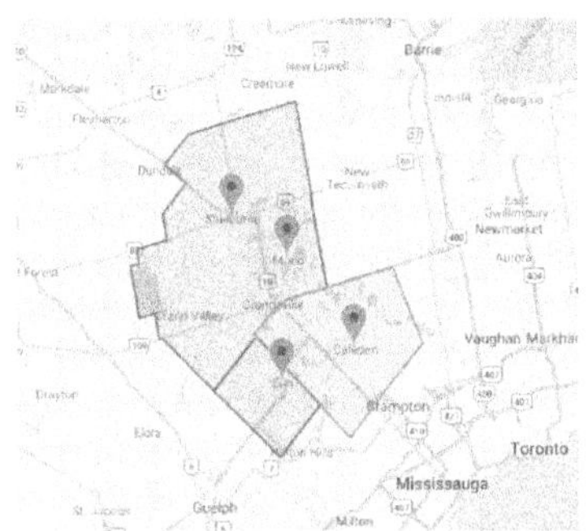

The Town of Mono
The Heart of the Headwaters

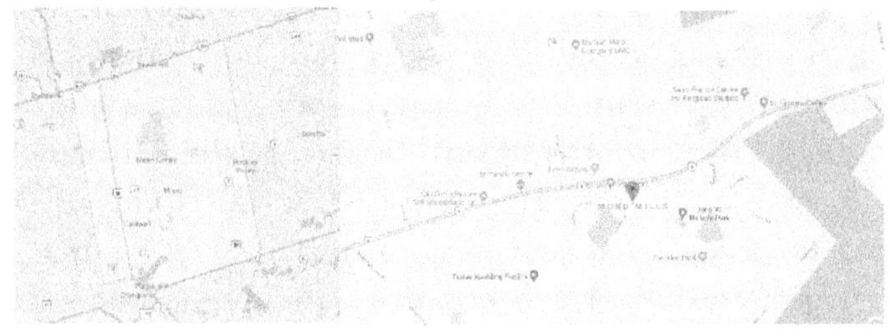

Start at page 29 of the Headwaters Visitors Guide to check out Mono Township and some of the wonderful things to do and see... and fall in love See everything this beautiful countryside has to offer on the online Headwaters Visitor Guide at Headwaters.ca

More stories in the
Love in the Hills of the Headwaters Series

REFUSING
TO
Expire

Love sometimes comes to us when we've completely given up on it. You just have to let go of the past and accept it.

Tori Campbell has neglected her needs as a woman, for far too long. Times are tough, money is tight, and raising three boys without a positive male role model in the house is challenging. After months of online dating, she realizes that there's a whole lot of crazy out there. Discouraged, she struggles to accept that she may spend the rest of her life alone. Roger Ford hasn't been lucky in love, so far. He's looking for someone to share his life. Someone to laugh and dance with. The moment they meet and he gazes into her enchanting, green eyes, he falls hard. Everything just seems to *fit*. Well, almost everything.

Roger may not be the perfect man, but he is no quitter, and he's determined to prove it.